PUPPET GRAVEYARD

by Tim Curran

1

Five months after her sister Gloria disappeared, Kitty Seevers got out of the shower in time to hear a pounding at the front door. Throwing on a robe and wrapping her hair in a towel, she rushed downstairs to find the FedEx guy standing there. He looked amused by her appearance as if a situation like that had played often enough times in his private fantasies.

After signing his clipboard, she took the registered letter from him. "Thanks," she said.

"No, thank *you*," he said.

Sighing, she shut the door and plopped herself on the couch. She had no idea who could be sending her a letter. Or why. The white cardboard envelope was sealed with packing tape and she had to use a scissors to cut it free. Inside were two things. The first raised an eyebrow. It was just a perfectly ordinary sheet of note paper folded in half. On it, printed in something of a shaky script were the words: BAMBOO LOUNGE, WICKER PARK. The second item made her heart drop in her chest. In a plastic baggie, there was a lock of hair. Perfectly golden hair with red highlights. It was Gloria's hair. There was no doubt in her mind.

She could have called the Chicago police and told them about it, but they'd been little help five months before, insinuating that Gloria was an attractive girl and attractive girls tended to get themselves in *situations*. And maybe that was true, but regardless of what situation she might have gotten into, Gloria would call. Because that was the kind of person Gloria was.

No, not the police. Kitty decided she wasn't putting up with *that* shit again. She would handle this herself as she should have right from the start.

So, five minutes later, she was on her laptop booking a flight to Chicago.

2

Ronny M. and Piggy were working the crowd, giving the audience exactly what they expected. Which, went a little something like this:

"Hey, Piggy?" Ronny said. "What's this I hear about you getting married?"

Piggy laughed. A mechanical, rapid-fire sound. "You don't miss much, do you, sunshine?" he said in a high, scratching voice. "Romance, you know, that's my thing. Kind of like naked bodybuilders and crack are you wife's thing. Ho!"

A few peals of laughter out in the crowd.

"Okay, now. Enough," Ronny said. He had Piggy balanced on his knee, his arm up the back of his suit coat. He held him as if he was afraid he might get away. "Enough of that."

Piggy snickered. "Enough of that? That's my problem, Ronny-boy, I can't get enough of *that*. I don't want to brag here, but only a litter box has seen more pussy than yours truly."

"Well, these good people don't want to hear about it, Piggy."

Piggy sat there on Ronny's knee in a cranberry velvet suit coat with an unlit cigarette in his hand. His head swiveled on his neck as he studied the crowd through the haze of cigarette smoke. "Hey, maybe you're right, Ronny. Maybe we don't want to get too personal here. We start that, I might have to admit a few things."

Ronny raised an eyebrow. "What sort of things, Piggy?"

"Well, I might have to admit to the fat guy in the first row that I banged his girlfriend last night." Piggy winked. "And let me tell you, buddy, your girl is like Maxwell House coffee—good to the last drop."

The fat man was red-faced, laughing so hard he started coughing.

Piggy said, "But between you and me, fella, that girl of yours...what's her name?"

"Sue," he managed. "Her name is Sue."

"Well, Sue there, you wanna be careful of her, pal. I mean, let's not dance around it here. She's got more crabs than a seafood salad. She's smoked more sausage than Jimmy Dean."

"All right, Piggy," Ronny said, smiling at the man apologetically.

The crowd roared out in the dimness of the Bamboo Lounge, hands clapping. A few drunks whistled. This is what they wanted. This is what they came night after night to see: Ronny M. and Piggy. Ventriloquist acts were a dime a dozen...but these two? Priceless.

"Now tell me about your marriage," Ronny prompted.

"Well, I met a girl, Ronny. I thought she was something special."

"Oh, really, why was that?"

"Well, Christ, she could suck a banana out without breaking the peel."

"Okay, Piggy, okay."

More laughter. Drunks repeating the one-liners out in the crowd. That was always a sure sign the routine was working.

"Okay nothing," Piggy said. "And what're you doing with your hand back there?"

"Well, I'm just touching your back."

"Well you keep it on my back and off my ass. Just because I'm sitting on your knee doesn't mean I want to play altar boy with you."

"Really, Piggy. You'll offend the audience."

"Offend them? Those lowlifes? Ha! That would be like offending a toilet by taking a shit in it." Piggy let go with his staccato laughter again. "I hate to be the one to tell you, Ronny-boy, but this place is a dump."

"Please, Piggy. You'll get us fired…"

"Fired? In this joint? That'd be like getting kicked out of a whorehouse for exposing yourself." Piggy leaned forward, put a hand to the side of his mouth. "I do apologize for Ronny here, folks. He's an ass-kisser from way back."

"I am not."

"Oh, but you are."

"Well, Mr. Collins hired us. I think he deserves some respect."

"Respect is one thing, Ronny, but kissing ass is another. Your head's so far up Collins' ass, every time he smiles I see your teeth. It's true, folks. Ronny here is so far up Collins' back door, he's sucking eyeball."

The crowd was eating it up raw and with both hands. Laughing like they would never stop. And the staff—waitresses, bartenders—were doubled over, loving some good ribbing and particularly at their boss's expense.

"Okay, Piggy, now tell me about your girl."

"Quit rushing me, Ronny."

"I'm not rushing you, Piggy."

"Hell, you aren't." Piggy was looking at him now, staring. "You don't want to piss me off, do you, Ronny? That's not what you want to do…is it?"

Ronny looked uncomfortable. He shifted on his wooden stool, like maybe this was going in the wrong direction, but he couldn't stop it. As if maybe he wasn't piloting this ship.

"No, of course not, Piggy. It's just that, well, these people are here for a good laugh."

"So, unzip your pants already. Jesus Christ."

The laughter out there was nervous, uneven.

Piggy looked out at the audience. "You people ever seen a guy like this? I swear to God, Ronny, sometimes I think the best part of you ran down your uncle's leg."

The laughter boomed now, the crowd figuring it was all part of the act. A set-up for the gags and one-liners.

"Now what about your girl," Ronny said in a guarded voice, as if he was afraid to set the dummy off again.

Piggy nodded. "Right. Well, I asked her about her giner and she told me it was tight as a drum. Problem was, it had an opening like one, too. This girl had more wang in her than a Chinese phonebook. I was tempted to shove a couple lemons up there, to pucker that stuff back up. Ah, but she was a good kid, you know? You leave out the biker clubs and football teams, the OPEN ALL NIGHT tattoo on her left thigh, she was real class…"

3

The guy outside the corridor leading to the dressing rooms was cracking his knuckles, working those hands which were big enough to drive tent-stakes through hard-packed clay. He stood there in his blue serge suit, bald head reflecting the stage lights, totally impervious. To the drunks, the noise, the buxom girl shaking her tits on stage.

When he saw Kitty coming, he frowned, placed his hands on his hips and shook his head. He took her by the arm and pulled her into the corridor and shut the door behind them so he could hear himself think.

"Listen, we go through this shit every night, you and I. It's getting old," he said to her, that big mitt still on her arm. "Now I'm going to tell you, honey, what I tell you every night: Mr. McBane and his dummy don't want any company. All that shit on stage...it's just an act, okay? They're not looking for followers."

Kitty bristled, pulled her arm away. She was small and fine-boned, thin as a peach twig...but about 110 pounds of poison if you pissed her off. "And I'll explain to *you* one last time that I only want to talk to Mr. McBane. Nothing more."

"Listen, honey, I think the guy's married and the boss here, he don't like anybody playing around in the dressing rooms. That's not the kind of place we run."

Kitty tried not to laugh. No, the Bamboo Lounge was strictly a class act. All those drunks out there had royal pedigrees and the strippers on stage wouldn't be turning tricks after lights out. "You listen to me," she said with venom. "And you listen good. I'm not a groupie. I only want to interview Mr. McBane for my college magazine. I'm a drama major and this is my assignment. It'll take ten minutes. Now why don't you be a good boy and just ask the man if he's interested?"

The big man sighed, worn down. "You know, I've been in this business a lot of years, sweet thing. And in that time, I've gotten real good at reading people...and you? You're full of shit. You're not with any college rag. We both know it." He threw his hands up. "But if you'll quit crawling up my ass every night, I'll go ask the man. Just the once. And if he says no, that's it. I don't wanna see you tomorrow night or the next. I don't wanna see you again period...got it?"

Kitty smiled.

4

"I don't have much time," Ronny said when Kitty was brought in, the door shut behind her. "That was my last show and I have a late dinner date."

"Sure, he does," Piggy said from his trunk by the vanity, the lid open and one arm thrown over the side like he was taking a bath in there. "Ronny's got a date with his right hand. I keep telling him it's not really sex if you're by yourself, but he don't listen."

Kitty laughed.

Ronny McBane smiled thinly. "That'll be enough from you, Piggy."

Kitty sat down and explained briefly what she wanted while Ronny listened intently. He was a tall man, narrow and reedy, but handsome in an undernourished way like certain rock stars that had been hitting the needle. His hands were large, the fingers fine and delicate. The hands of a magician...or a ventriloquist. He liked to express himself with them freely.

"Well, I'll tell you what I can, Miss Seevers."

"Call me Kitty."

"*Meoooooowwww*," Piggy said. "Come here, Kitty, Kitty, Kitty..."

Ronny went over to him, picking him up. "I'm afraid he'll be impossible until you greet him properly."

9

Laughing, Kitty went over and extended her hand to Piggy. She was amazed how good Ronny was. Piggy's hand gripped her own. It was a cold grip, but oddly firm for a doll. Piggy bowed his head and kissed her fingers. When he was done he made a big show of raising his eyebrows and opening and closing his mouth, making smacking sounds. "You have fish for dinner or did you just have a little itch?"

"Oh!" Kitty gasped. "You're terrible."

"Ain't it the truth," Piggy said. "Ain't it just the truth."

Ronny set Piggy back in the box and they got down to business.

"Well, Kitty," he said, that thin smile touching his lips again. "Where should I begin? I have no formal training in theater or ventriloquism. I'm entirely self-taught. I made Piggy myself and took some years doing it…"

Kitty listened while he prattled on, making a show of keeping notes, nodding with enthusiasm at the right moments. But the notes were mostly doodling and what she was really doing was studying Ronny McBane's pale, dour face which was so tense and rigid it looked like it had been airbrushed onto the skull beneath. As he talked, the corners of his lips attempted the smile he emoted so well on stage. And it worked out there, but up close like this it was an upturned frown, rubbery and artificial. It never touched his eyes and their haunted depths.

It was hard to say who was more wooden…Ronny or Piggy.

"What made you get into the business?" Kitty asked.

Ronny McBane opened his mouth, but it was the dummy that did the talking. "Well, look at him, baby. He's a fucking wreck. A nervous wreck…aren't you a nervous wreck, Ronny? Afraid of his own shadow. If it wasn't for me holding his dick, he'd piss down his own leg."

Ronny tittered uneasily. The grin he offered Kitty was like an ax wound in a skull. "You keep quiet, Piggy."

Kitty swallowed dryly, felt something fluttering in her belly. "How...how can you make him talk like that? I mean, you're over here...but I saw his mouth move."

"Come a little closer, sweet meat, and I'll show you how it really moves," Piggy said.

The sexual innuendo went right over Kitty's head. What she was seeing...it could not be. She looked from Ronny McBane to his dummy, back again. It was a trick and she knew it was a trick, yet a gnawing chill expanded in her chest. Piggy sat there in his trunk, grinning like a death's-head, lewd and unpleasant. He had teeth, she saw, long yellow teeth, crooked and decayed.

Since when did dummies have teeth?

"How..." Kitty mumbled.

"A trick of the trade," Ronny said, looking frightened himself. But it was really hard to tell. There was so much barely-concealed torment slathered onto that face, maybe it was all her imagination.

She decided it was.

"You really had me going for a moment there," she said to Ronny, not Piggy, trying to sound relieved, but failing.

"You want to get going?" Piggy said. "Come over here, I'll get you going."

"Okay, Piggy," Ronny said. "We've had our laugh."

Kitty looked from her notes to Ronny's face, avoiding his eyes which were like windows looking into a crypt. "Is...um...is it generally just the two of you? Do you ever have another dummy involved in the act?"

"She's talking threesome here, Ronny."

Kitty feigned a laugh. "Oh, stop it. I'm serious."

"So am I, lady," the dummy said. "So am I."

"Never. No other dummies. Just the two of us," Ronny said.

"How about assistants? I heard you had an assistant."

Ronny's eyes went dark and stormy. "Once, yes. We had a...a woman working with us, but it didn't pan out."

Kitty could feel Piggy's eyes burning holes into her back, but of course they weren't really eyes, just marbles. Dead, inert marbles. Still...she could feel them, that vile gaze creeping over her skin. She turned and looked and, yes, Piggy was staring, mouth sprung open. But he was not moving.

Not at all.

When she looked back at Ronny, however, the dummy started talking again: "Maybe you ought to interview me, baby. Women make Ronny nervous, but I like 'em just fine...if you know what I mean."

Kitty laughed, not finding any of it funny now. She supposed all ventriloquists had unusual relationships with their dummies, used them to say things they were incapable of, but enough was enough. "Okay already, Mr. McBane. Why don't we let Piggy rest, put him in his box or something."

And again, that strident, unnerving voice from behind her: "Only box I want to get into is yours, baby."

"Okay. C'mon, now. This is all getting a little crude."

"The lady is right, Piggy."

Piggy cackled low and dusty, but kept his mouth shut.

And that was good, because the very sound of his voice was beginning to make Kitty's flesh crawl in slow waves. Maybe it was her, but the room seemed suddenly too close, too claustrophobic, too something. Like a coffin, narrow and moldering and airless.

"I can't help thinking I've met you before," Ronny said to her, fixing her with those eyes, that twisted mind behind them that could make dummies move from across the room.

"You've probably seen me in the audience," she said. "I rarely miss a show. Particularly since this assignment began."

"Yes, that must be it."

Piggy started laughing. "Oh, I don't think that's it at all. She looks like someone, Ronny…haven't you guessed who?"

Kitty slapped her notebook shut.

She had to get out of there, out of that damn confining room. It was like being trapped in the mind of a lunatic.

"Well, I want to thank you," she said. "Ha, both of you."

"Oh, the pleasure's been ours."

"It has," Piggy said. "And don't look so grim, chippy. You'll be seeing us again, maybe sooner than you think. Keep your window open, I might come into your bedroom some night. Then I'll show you some real tricks. You'd like that, wouldn't you?"

But Kitty was certain she would not have liked that at all.

There was something positively obscene about the dummy. The idea of it creeping into her room by moonlight was enough to make her teeth chatter.

She let herself out, Ronny staring intently at the floor.

After the door closed, she could hear the dummy laughing in there.

5

It took Kitty some time to come down after that.

Truth be told, she'd always found mannequins and dolls and puppets more than a little unnerving. Ventriloquist dummies topped the list because they talked. Their mouths opened and shut. Their eyes moved. But they were only wood and plastic animated by clever artifice. The real disturbing thing about the dummies were the ventriloquists themselves who created personalities for them, imbuing them with a disturbing half-life. Mostly, she knew, it was harmless. Just because they did this so effectively did not mean they were schizophrenic or suffering from multiple personality disorders. And it was only in the movies that the ventriloquist channeled his evil, subconscious, murderous desires into his dummy. That was comic book stuff.

This is what she kept telling herself.

But being that Gloria had worked with Ronny M. and Piggy just before she disappeared, Kitty didn't necessarily believe it. There was something strange about this act and something far stranger about a ventriloquist who could make his dummy not only talk from across the room, but *move*.

There was something here and she planned on finding out what.

6

Charlie Bascomb ran his agency out of a crumbling office building in the Loop. He was on the second floor, sandwiched in-between a cut-rate goldsmith and a sex novelty distributor. It wasn't a very good neighborhood and Kitty brought along a little .32 automatic in her purse.

You never knew these days.

There was no one in the outer office at the receptionist's desk, so Kitty went through a door marked PRIVATE. Right into the lair of Charlie Bascomb, a guy who'd once handled some real talent, but these days was barely making a living keeping the after-hours clubs supplied with strippers and low-rent stand-up acts.

He was on the phone when Kitty came in. He waved her into a chair. Charlie Bascomb was small and plump, but cagey-looking, predatory. He was arguing with someone about a band he was managing, saying that the days of ten percent cuts were history. All the real agencies hacked off twenty before they even looked at a client. A moment or two later, he slammed down the phone. "And what do you want?" he said.

"Your receptionist wasn't there, so I just walked in," Kitty told him.

Bascomb laughed. "She's out to lunch. Hell, even when she's here, she's out to lunch." He sighed, cleared a space on his desk for his hands. He looked Kitty up and down like a dog

15

deciding whether an available bone was worth chewing on. "Well, I'll tell you, honey. Your tits are too small for a dancer...but you're pretty, sultry even. You do any singing?"

Kitty laughed now herself. "I'm not here for representation, Mr. Bascomb. I have no talent, trust me."

"Neither do my clients," he admitted. "Okay, what do you want?"

Kitty sat there a moment, wondering that very question herself. "I understand you used to handle ventriloquists."

Bascomb stared at her long and hard. "I did, but I don't anymore." He lit a cigarette, fanned the smoke away with his hand. "I'm not sure what your interest is in this, Miss—"

"Seevers, Kitty Seevers."

"—Seevers, but I don't mind saying between you and me and the clock on the wall, that those ventriloquists are a strange bunch. Temperamental is a word for them and so is crazy."

Kitty nodded. "I'm actually interested in one act in particular."

"Oh? And which one is that?"

"Ronny M. and Piggy."

Bascomb sat there looking at her. Looking at her and *through* her like he could see the doorway beyond right through her head. He was ruddy-faced, pink-cheeked...but the mention of those names drained all the color from him. He leaned back in his chair, that crooked smile locked on his lips. You would have needed a chisel to get it off. He brought his cigarette to his lips and his hand was shaking.

"Mr. Bascomb?"

He swallowed, kept swallowing. He looked like he'd just been told there was a tumor eating away his guts. "Who," he began, trying to regulate his breathing, "who sent you here? Tell me who it was."

Kitty held up her hands. "No one. I just came because—"

"Because why?" The fear or shock was gone now, what was left behind was something like anger, like hatred. "You tell me who the fuck sent you!"

Kitty thought he was going to come right over the desk at her. "Listen, Mr. Bascomb...nobody sent me. I don't know what you're getting so riled about...I just came to ask a few questions about an act."

That seemed to soothe him. He pulled off his cigarette, breathing hard. "Yeah, I used to handle McBane and I don't anymore. And that's all I got to say on the matter."

But Kitty hadn't come this far to back away now.

What she needed here was bait.

So, she laid it out for him, knowing she'd have to put her cards on the table, confess before she'd get a confession. "I'm looking for my sister, Mr. Bascomb. She was Ronny McBane's assistant. That's all I know. She disappeared five months ago and I'd like to know why."

Bascomb softened. "Did you go to the police?"

"Oh yes, several times. But there's nothing there. It's not like they found her body or anything. She just disappeared, cleaned out her things at the room she was staying in and became a statistic."

"And you think McBane had something to do with it?"

"Yes," Kitty said. "Maybe I'm wrong, but something tells me I'm not."

Bascomb stared off into space. "Well, I'm sorry for your sister. I really am. But what do you want from me? I haven't handled McBane in three years, closer to four."

"Tell me about him," Kitty said. "You might be the only one who can."

It was obvious that Bascomb didn't like the idea at all. There was something there, bad blood maybe. "Okay...I mean, shit, I suppose it's time to tell somebody. Answer me something first...have you seen McBane? Have you talked to him?"

It was Kitty's turn to look frightened. "Yes, I have."

"And?"

She chewed her lower lip, picking her words carefully. "Honestly? He and that dummy scared the hell out of me. There's something wrong there, something real wrong."

"Oh, you're damn right, sister, there sure as hell *is* something wrong there." Bascomb paused, lit another cigarette off the butt of the last. "What I tell you...it stays between you and me, understand?"

Kitty promised him it would.

"Okay, all right then. Now, like you probably already know, I handled ventriloquist acts for years. Dozens of 'em. Some good and, well, some not so good. My uncle could throw his voice and my old man made dummies and puppets, that sort of thing...so I know the business backwards and forwards. Ain't a lot I don't know about ventriloquism. Now, most people think vent artists are nuts and some of them definitely are. But for most it's just a gag, a neat trick they can pull off. End of the day, they put their dummy in a trunk and that's that. Then there are the other kind..."

Bascomb said that some ventriloquists were natural introverts, quiet as mice, but when they had dummies on their laps they channeled all their repressed thoughts and secret desires through the things. Made their dummies do and say things they would never dream of saying or doing in a million years. Those were the dangerous ones, the ones that developed a personality so strong for their dummy that often it overpowered their own. It became a symbiotic relationship, one feeding off the other. Without the ventriloquist, the dummy was just a piece of wood...but without the dummy, the ventriloquist was trapped by his own inhibitions.

"Codependency is what I'm saying here, Miss Seevers," Bascomb told her. "And like a codependency in the real world, sometimes it's beneficial and other times…well, destructive. I knew a vent artist who slit his wrists when somebody stole his dummy. Can you imagine what it must have been like for that guy? Like somebody had stolen half of his mind, half of his soul."

Bascomb let that sink in for a moment, then went on to explain the mechanics of dummies themselves. "Vent dolls are an art form. These days, most guys buy 'em straight off the rack same way they would a suit. There's companies that mass produce 'em. But in the old days, vent artists would make their own to start with until they could afford a guy like my old man who was a craftsman. Every dummy my old man made was a custom job, handmade of the best materials—hardwood joints, brass mechanisms, aluminum return springs, oak headsticks, glass eyes and shell winkers. The vent told my old man exactly what he wanted and got his money's worth. One-of-a-kind vent dummies we're talking here. Priceless in their own way.

"Yeah, my old man was one of the great figure artists, right up there with Frank Marshall and the McElroy brothers. All of his figures had at least thirteen or more animations…so, you get the picture, I know dummies. I know a good one and I know a bad one…and Ronny McBane's dummy, Piggy? That one's in a class all by itself. I've never seen such articulation in my life."

Bascomb told Kitty that Piggy seemed almost human at times and very often, Ronny seemed less than that. There was a symbiosis there, too, but a bad one. Maybe something more along the lines of parasitism. Bascomb managed Ronny's act for two years and it nearly cost him his sanity. He had heard of performers arguing with their dummies, had seen it once or twice, but never anything like this business with Ronny and Piggy. The arguments often got very ugly with Piggy running down Ronny to the point of being vicious. It was unpleasant to imagine, but positively unsettling to actually witness. Bascomb said it got to the point where you were thinking that Piggy was the master and Ronny was the puppet.

"I've seen some screwed up ventriloquist/dummy relationships in my time—knew a guy once who slept with his dummy, kept it there in bed with him when he was doing it with a woman—but the Ronny/Piggy thing was far worse, I tell you." Bascomb paused, dragged off his cigarette. "If you talked with McBane, then I'm betting Piggy was there. Ronny doesn't go anywhere without him and maybe it's the other way around, who can say? But if you did, then you might have noticed some...*funny* things about that dummy, maybe how it moves when Ronny's nowhere near it."

Kitty told him she'd seen that, all right. "It was weird...it gave me the creeps. How can he do that?"

Bascomb shrugged. "You tell me. I've seen some good gags in my time, but this is something else entirely. I had a guy, a good vent artist, tell me it wasn't possible. That the only way Ronny could do that was by using his mind, telekinesis or one of them Stephen King things. I don't know. But I'll tell you, I'll tell you in all honesty...there's something unnatural about Piggy."

But Kitty didn't need to be told that.

She'd never forget what she saw in that dressing room. The look in the dummy's eyes, wicked and sadistic and completely evil. That was crazy thinking, sure, but it was exactly what she had thought at the time: Piggy was not just a wooden figure, but something sentient...and not altogether sane.

Bascomb said that Ronny was real strange about it all. He mothered Piggy and Piggy could barely tolerate Ronny's presence. You couldn't have imagined a more clear cut case of split personality.

"One time, oh shit, one time McBane had a bad show. I don't know what happened exactly, but things just never got off the ground. He couldn't get the chemistry going between himself and Piggy...I mean, you know, between those personalities of his. Things got nasty out there and it was not funny, I'll tell you that much. Piggy was running him down, telling the fucking audience—excuse my French here—the worse things you could imagine about Ronny...that he was a mama's boy, that he had some kind of mannequin that he masturbated over. Shit, it was bad. Real bad. Embarrassing, downright spooky. Because, you know, the people out in the audience, they figured Ronny had snapped, using the dummy to sort of mentally castrate himself...but me? I wasn't so sure by that point. I wasn't so sure of anything.

"So, the show ended, thank God. The management was crawling up my ass and it was hard all around. But Ronny still had another show to do in an hour or so...two shows a night, that's how it worked. Well, the owners told me that if Ronny pulled that shit again, they were calling for the guys in the white suits. It was that goddamn bad. So, I went to the dressing room to check on my boy..." Bascomb paused here and it wasn't for effect. His complexion had a yellowish tint to it, his eyes filled with pain. "I...well, I went into the dressing room, right? I mean, I walked right in there and Ronny's on the couch, eyes closed, breathing deep and even. Looks like he's asleep. I would have sworn he was asleep. There was blood all over his hand and arm...I looked closer and, Jesus, I could see *teeth marks* embedded into his wrist. Some of them had broken the skin and I thought, oh Christ, Ronny has really slipped the old peg now, he's biting himself. And that's when I noticed Piggy was sitting up in a chair in the corner, in the shadows. His...his eyes were open and shining and he started talking. He said to me, he said,

21

You better get the fuck out of here before you piss me off...before I start telling you things about yourself you don't wanna hear..."

Bascomb was shaking badly after that.

Some confessions were good for the soul, but others were destructive and dangerous. This one was one of those.

He had to use both hands to light another cigarette. His lips were gray and twisted like two dead worms pressed together. "I know...I know Ronny must have been awake, must have been screwing around with me, but I wasn't sure, I just wasn't sure. I started getting whacko ideas that maybe Piggy had bitten him, disciplined him for making a mess of the performance. But dummies...they don't bite people, do they? I mean, no, they don't have teeth and they couldn't bite if they wanted to...because...because they're only dummies...right?"

Kitty sat there, something white and cold in her vitals. She wanted to tell him, yes, dummies are just dummies...but she wasn't so sure anymore herself. She wasn't so sure of a lot of things. And teeth? Yes, Piggy had teeth. Long teeth like the Big Bad Wolf. Awful, crooked teeth.

She'd seen them.

Bascomb seemed to recover after a moment. "Oh, I could go on and tell you other things, things that would turn your hair white. Shit about that dummy, about Piggy...well, none of it's good. Far as I'm concerned, Ronny McBane is insane. And Piggy? Well, that's something I don't want to think about more than I absolutely have to. Now, I don't know the full picture here, but I do know that there's something spooky about the McBanes themselves. I've picked up bits and pieces, hard not to, and what I heard I didn't like. Suffice to say that Ronny's mother was some kind of fanatic and I've heard stories about him being abused and the like. Bits about Ronny having a brother and sister who died under some pretty suspicious circumstances."

Kitty sighed, soaking it all in and beginning to wonder—and not for the first time—just exactly what she was getting herself into here. This wasn't merely some crazy ventriloquist and his dummy, this was something more. Something that had a history, something that was black and tangled at its roots.

"Is the mother still living?" she asked.

"No." Bascomb stopped there, hesitated, maybe wondering if he should go any further. He looked decidedly older than he had when he began talking. "What I'm going to tell you here is just…well, it's second-hand stuff. I can't really corroborate any of it." He paused again, licked his lips with a tongue dry as a strop. "Apparently, the mother was murdered…well, at least, she died violently. That's how the story goes. They found her in bed a few years before I took the act on. She lived alone, no cats or dogs, yet they found her all mauled and mangled. Bitten up. Something had torn her throat out and from what I hear, whatever it was, it took its time."

Kitty wanted to know more, grisly as it all was. What had been at the old woman? What had been chewing on her? But she could see from the look on Bascomb's face that he was playing it straight with her; he was telling all he knew. When he was done, he dismissed it all with a wave of his hand, but there was something in his eyes…something very frightened.

He went on to tell her that while he managed Ronny and Piggy, he got word that they were having problems with some caretaker out at Harvest Hill Cemetery. No, Ronny had not admitted it to him, but Bascomb had heard, all right. When you manage an act, when you pour your blood, sweat, and tears into something like that, you find out things. Apparently, this caretaker was having problems with Ronny and the dummy. They would go into the family crypt at night to visit dear old dead mom. Far into the wee hours of the morning they could be heard in there—Ronny and Piggy—shouting and singing and shrieking out things to the dead woman. The caretaker described what went on in there as being "profane." Which, Bascomb fully admitted, was a pretty arbitrary term when you came down to it. It depended entirely on the user.

"Did you find out what that was?" Kitty asked.

"No and yes. Ronny wasn't defiling her or her coffin if that's what you were thinking, but the conversations in there…well, that combined with the racket of them fighting and screaming, it was just bad. The caretaker said he found blood in the crypt after they left…Ronny's, I suppose."

He told her about Eddie Bose.

"Eddie was a good kid, a real perfectionist, you know? He was one of the best vent artists on the circuit," Bascomb explained. "Well, he took a real interest in Ronny and Piggy. He knew what he was seeing and what that dummy was capable of was, well, not right. And he was an expert, he knew all the tricks. As you can imagine, Ronny being the way he is, he did not want another ventriloquist around. But Eddie wasn't about to give up that easy…"

He was expected to go to the top of the business and maybe he would have if he'd left things lie. But it wasn't his way. Ronny's dummy was like no other and Eddie planned out finding out how and why. If there was a secret there, a revolutionary mechanism that made Piggy do the things he did, then Eddie had to know what it was. What ventriloquist wouldn't? Bascomb said that Eddie began following Ronny and the dummy around. Ronny didn't let Piggy out of his sight, but sooner or later, he would have to. He would have to sleep. And when that happened, Eddie planned on borrowing Piggy and finding out what made him tick.

"He trailed them back to an old, rotting house up in Edgewater," Bascomb said, his voice worn now. "That's what Eddie did. It was Ronny's mother's house…some big old mausoleum they should have torn down years before. The perfect sort of place, I guess, for true madness to have free reign. Well, make a long story short, one night Eddie forced a window and went in there. He wasn't in there long, but what he saw, Miss Seevers, what Eddie looked upon in there…well, it ruined him."

Kitty tensed. "What do you mean?"

Bascomb studied his hands, exhaled through his nostrils. "Eddie just dropped out of the scene. No more gigs, nothing. Well, shit, the kid had real talent and he also had a lot of friends working the vent racket. People had a lot of questions. So, well, I tracked him down. It took weeks, but I found him in a dive downtown. I barely recognized him. He was a good-looking kid, I tell you. But what I found in that bar…well, it scared me. Scared me bad. He was thin and spindly, shaking so badly he could barely suck down the whiskey there. Eddie had jet-black hair last time I saw him and at that bar? Well, there were white streaks in it. He wasn't even thirty and he looked sixty, face full of lines, the left side paralyzed or something. It was hanging loose as a hound dog's jowls…except down at the corner of his mouth, it was pulled up into this horrible grin like something a corpse might wear. This toothy, sardonic grin that made my guts go to sauce. I asked him if he was all right, if he needed a doctor or something, but he told me flat out that he'd never be all right again…"

Bascomb was thinking he'd suffered a stroke and maybe a nervous breakdown to boot. And he was right on both counts. For Eddie Bose had seen something in the McBane house…something so gruesome, so harrowing, that the very shock of it had physically and mentally deranged him.

Bascomb was deadly pale now and his lips were thick, rubbery like they were numb. He seemed to be having trouble getting them to form the words his brain told them needed to be said: "So there I was in that dirty, stinking place with Eddie Bose…or something that had once been Eddie Bose…and dear God, the look in his eyes. They had seen things, Miss Seevers, shown Eddie things that had shattered his mind.

"I asked him what in the hell happened. And he told me. He told me pretty much what I've just told you…that he was obsessed with learning the secret of Piggy, that he'd broke into that house. I asked him what he'd seen there and I knew right then that whatever it was it had stripped the cogs of his brain, stripped them smooth. He looked over at me and those eyes were like holes burned straight through into hell and he asked me, straight out asked me, if I thought it was possible that dummies, ventriloquist dummies, could be *possessed*. That was the word he used. Possessed, you know, like that kid in that movie. Possessed, Eddie said, by things nameless, things dead, things inhuman. His words. Was that possible? Could some evil intelligence make a vent dummy that was kept in a coffin filled with black, wormy grave earth sit up and smile, start talking to you in the tormented voices of your mother and father…*both of whom were long dead.*"

Bascomb didn't say anything after that for a time.

He slouched in his chair, looking gray and old and milked dry. He smoked and stared at the wall and Kitty said nothing herself, maybe afraid of what she would have said if she opened her mouth. She'd been raised Catholic and she understood the politics of spirit possession as well as the next. But what Bascomb was saying…what Eddie Bose had told him…well, it all took it to a different level, now didn't it? It made something beyond the boundaries of belief into a cackling, infectious lunacy. Kitty was practical in all things, but she could not laugh this off. What was rotting inside of Bascomb was rotting in her now, too.

"What happened to him…to Eddie?" she finally asked, knowing it was a mistake.

"What happened?" Bascomb chuckled mirthlessly. "He died. He died hard, Miss Seevers, he died horribly."

"What…what happened to him?"

Bascomb shook his head slowly from side to side, looking at his hands again. "I was worried about him. We were *all* worried about him. One night, I went up to the cold water flat he was living in. The door was open. I was the first one to see his body. There was blood…Christ in Heaven, there was blood everywhere. I've never seen that much. Eddie…*Eddie* was all broken-up and twisted-looking, like a doll some kid got tired of and stomped under foot. That's how he looked. And his face…oh, Jesus, hitched into this pathetic grimace like a great, jagged rip in vinyl. Looking like that, well, I figured he'd been so scared of something he'd screamed himself to death. But you know what was even worse than that? You wanna know what I see when I close my eyes at night? His *eyes*. I see his eyes looking out at me, wide open, glassy like marbles, black and empty and filled with a dread, an insane horror that's beyond pain, beyond agony, beyond anything you can imagine…yes, that's what I saw in Eddie's flat."

Kitty felt something bunch in her stomach. Bascomb's fright was real and she felt it, too, felt it moving through her, scarring her in places that would never properly heal. And the crazy, impossible thing was that she could see those eyes of Eddie Bose in her mind, too, hysterical and neurotic, filled with an absolute mindless terror.

The coroner said that Eddie died of heart failure and had been gnawed on by rats, post mortem. But Bascomb didn't believe it, didn't believe a word of it. For he saw some of the bite marks on Eddie and no rat born ever had a set of teeth like that. So, he came up with his own cause of death…Eddie Bose died of heart failure, yes, but it was brought upon by something biting him relentlessly until his mind—what there was left of it—was drawn into some sucking gray pit of dementia.

"What did you do?" Kitty put to him.

"What in the hell could I do? The authorities closed the book, but I was far from done. I loved Eddie. Before that obsession slit his mind open, he was a really good guy." Bascomb brushed cigarette ashes off his pants. "Well, first thing I did was the stupidest thing I could think of. And that's why where Eddie's troubles left off, mine began."

Kitty waited for it, wondering when this daisy chain of mania would end. And what, when all was confessed, she would think of it.

"After we buried Eddie, I guess it was my turn to go fucking nuts," Bascomb said, clenching his left fist in his right, maybe remembering something he'd done with it or should have done. "My old man never said I was the brightest light on the tree, so true to form, my belly full of hate, I went after Ronny. Yes, that's what I did. He'd come up to my office to sign some papers. Piggy was with him, but packed away in his trunk out in the hallway. I went up one side of Ronny and down the other. What in the name of fuck, I said to him, did you do to Ronny Bose? You and that half-ass goddamn puppet of yours?"

Bascomb fully admitted he was more than a little wound-up from grief and rage and the still-simmering horror of what had become of Eddie Bose. He probably had no right to jump all over Ronny McBane like that. Sure, Ronny was flakier than a box of instant potatoes, wasn't playing with a full deck—shit, he was missing more than one major suit—but he was only dangerous to himself, ultimately. Well, Ronny, that poor, pitiful bastard, looked like he was going to start crying on the spot. He started yammering on in this pathetic little voice that belonged to a scolded schoolboy, said it wasn't his fault, God knew he'd tried to keep Eddie away, tried to talk him out of his damnable curiosity…but what happened at the house, there was nothing he could do. Eddie came to see things and he had seen them, all right.

Bascomb shook his head. "He was ranting and raving, saying it wasn't his fault and that I better keep my mouth shut, to leave well enough alone, because if Piggy found out…well, there were things the dummy could do, awful things. And about that time, Piggy woke up…I mean, *Ronny* started throwing his voice, saying muffled things from inside that box. I didn't hear what they were, but I could hear the tone of his voice…and I knew I had just stepped into some shit I'd never be able to rub off my shoe. And I was right. Regardless, I told Ronny I was done with him and I was done with goddamn ventriloquists in general and that he could take his fucked-up act and that ugly little freak he called a dummy and shove him up his ass sideways."

Down deep, Bascomb was more than a little afraid of Ronny's madness and Piggy in general by that point. And he knew he had woken a dragon by pissing all over the Gruesome Twosome (as he called them). Something was going to happen, he knew, and then it did.

Bascomb butted his cigarette and stared at Kitty with eyes smoldering with hopelessness. "It started when my dog got killed. He was a little cocker spaniel and Meg and I, we couldn't have kids, so we put all our love into that little mutt." He paused, eyes misting. He brushed them dry with the back of his fist. "I came home one night and that little dog—Homer, we called him—was on the porch, his little head nearly twisted off. His eyes were gone…I…I could see by the marks there that they'd been bitten out or carved out. Jesus. About that time, the phone started ringing in the dead of night. I'd answer it and there'd be no one there…but I knew there was someone.

Someone or something. After a second or two, I'd hear someone breathing...but not any normal kind of obscene phone caller breathing, but a horrible hollow sound like air sucked through a reed. Then the laughter would start...that scratching, scraping laughter of Piggy's. Night after night it would be like that.

"Maybe, maybe I should have went to the police. I don't know. If it wasn't Piggy laughing, it was just the sound of chattering teeth. Chattering, snapping...believe me, you cannot imagine anything as scary as that: answering the phone at three in the morning and hearing that breathing, those chattering teeth."

Bascomb said he was terrified.

Not just for himself, but for his wife, Meg. She was a sweet kid, he said, the sort of patient, loving, devoted wife a bum like him had no business having. Bascomb moved them into another house out in the suburbs, had the phone number unlisted. It worked, at least for a month or so, but soon enough, it began again. The phone calls. The chattering teeth. The laughter. It was building into something just as it had with the dog and he damn well knew it, he just didn't know what to do about it. At night, sometimes there were faint tapping or clawing sounds at the doors...scratching sounds at the windows. But there was never anything there when he looked. One morning, his car—brand new customized Buick Regal— had been vandalized. There were deep scratches running from the front quarter panel to the back, on the trunk and hood, the doors. Deep ruts that had peeled the paint down to metal like a garden trowel had been dragged across it. The cops said it was kids. Kids out looking for kicks. That he should keep his car in the garage, damn kids these days.

But it wasn't kids and Bascomb knew it.

Just like he knew the claw marks on the front door weren't from dogs and the sounds he heard at night were not mice. He would wake up, hear the sound of footsteps, light but audible footsteps coming up the stairs, tapping sounds on the walls and more than once, the chattering of teeth out in the corridor. But he never had the balls to open the bedroom door and see what it was. The stress of it all was taking a toll on him, and Meg and he were fighting something awful—he wanted to move again, but she adamantly refused. It got so bad Meg started sleeping in the spare bedroom.

Bascomb paused, dredging up all the cold filth of his soul now, then went on in a broken, delirious voice: "One night I woke up and I just knew the worst had happened, I knew it. I could feel it in the air, that my world had just gone stark raving mad. I rushed down the hallway and I saw Meg on the spare bed, sprawled out like she'd been dropped from fifty feet up. And I saw, I saw..." Bascomb's breath was coming in short, sharp gasps now and his eyes were rolling madly. "...I...oh Jesus...oh God in Heaven, I saw, I saw someone bending over her. Except it wasn't someone, but *Piggy*...his eyes lit up like full moons, that terrible black grin on his narrow dummy face. He was doing something to Meg, those skinny hands pressed over her mouth and nose...he was suffocating her. I made to rush him, to tear him into kindling, but then he started speaking...speaking in the voice of Eddie Bose, a shrieking voice telling me how Eddie was in hell, how he was trapped in hell..."

Kitty tried everything she could to calm Bascomb down, for his face was hooked in a leering mask, his eyes wide and dark and wet, but he shrugged her off. "Maybe...maybe I passed out...I don't know, I don't fucking now...fainted or something. When I woke up the dummy was gone and Meg...oh my poor baby, my goddamn wife...her face was twisted up in a sneer, all blue and black and bloated, her tongue hanging from her mouth and her eyes bulging from her head..." Bascomb broke into tears and shuddered, crying into his hands. When he recovered, he lit a cigarette, looking pinched and bloodless and wan like somebody who'd just battled a deadly disease. "The police said she asphyxiated, that she simply stopped breathing probably due to some undiagnosed involuntary motor defect. That was that. But I'll tell you in all honesty, Miss Seevers, I died that day, too. I was broken by what I saw, by having my life destroyed before my very eyes. Yes, Piggy pulled out my soul, spit on it, fouled it, then put it back inside me and told me to go and live with myself."

Kitty was stunned, breathless, her brain full of shadows and shapes and crawling things. She wasn't honestly sure who was more crazy—Bascomb and his tales of vengeful living dummies or herself for believing every word of it. Somebody was screwy here and she was pretty sure it was both of them.

Bascomb blew out a column of smoke. "But that was years ago and I probably hallucinated it all, don't you think?" He laughed at the idea, as if trying to convey to Kitty that you could talk yourself into just about anything after a time. "And now you come to me and say your sister is missing and maybe Ronny McBane had something to do with it. I'd say you're probably right. I feel for you and I feel for your sister and that's why I'm telling you now not to turn a tragedy into a catastrophe. Ronny McBane told me to leave well enough alone and I should have. God help me, but I should have. And now I'm asking you to do the same thing."

"But..."

"Walk away, honey. For the love of God, just walk away from this while you still can. There's things at work here. Things you can't understand."

And what could Kitty say to that?

Nothing and that's exactly what she said. She thanked Bascomb for his time and left, thinking she was losing her mind now, too. And behind her, Bascomb was sobbing, all his options run out and his life stolen from him along with his sanity.

7

What now?
What came next?

What was Kitty to do armed with this new, impossible knowledge? Sitting in her hotel room that night she told herself that she was not going to turn away from this. That if she swallowed what Bascomb had said, then she might as well go check herself into the madhouse right now. Because, really, that's what it all was: madness. Sure, Bascomb was completely convinced of what he was saying and Kitty had been, too…you couldn't sit there and listen to that nightmare pouring out of him without feeling its effects, without finding yourself drawn down into some fathomless blackness.

But now that she was back in the real world, her thinking mind had questions.

There's a common thread to all this and it has nothing to do with spooks. Bascomb needs therapy. He's crazy. That entire Eddie Bose situation must have unhinged him in ways he wasn't even aware of, she thought. *That's got to be it. Whether Bose ever told him any of that business about spirits and possession is open to conjecture. Regardless, it unhinged him. He let his mind direct all its shock, trauma, and sense of loss at Ronny and the dummy and their twisted, unhealthy relationship. He needed to find a target for his despair and that was Piggy. By that point he'd already talked himself into the idea that it was some evil devil doll. But it was delirium, mania. That's all.*

Yet…despite her very rational turn of mind, she wasn't entirely convinced. If Bascomb was telling her the truth about the midnight sessions in the family crypt, then there was definitely something weird and downright scary going on with Ronny McBane. That he wasn't right in the head, she knew from her interview with him, and that he had some inexplicable power over the dummy she had seen firsthand. But that didn't necessitate anything supernatural. Something was going on here and that common thread led to the disappearance of her sister. But she wasn't about to believe that Ronny McBane was anything more than deranged and Piggy was anything more than a dummy.

Now it was time to turn up the heat and dig a little deeper.

She'd hired a private investigator three days before and now it was time to find out what he had learned. And when she did, she'd act on it because that's the kind of person she was. Her sister Gloria was hardly an angel. Kitty knew some of the dirt and it was pretty much the same old shopworn dirt that came with the entertainment business…but that did not make Gloria a bad person.

Whatever had happened to her, she deserved better.

She deserved to be more than a statistic in the police files.

Kitty took out her cell and looked through her photos. *Gloria, Gloria, Gloria.* Funny, as a kid, she'd been so jealous of her she sometimes broke out in hives and now she languished over her sister's photos on a daily basis. Gloria was older than she and far prettier. Just ask anyone. Maybe mom would never admit as such, in so many words, but Gloria got the attention because she not only looked good but looked good *regardless* of what she was doing. Peeling potatoes, doing the dishes…it didn't matter: she had looks, grace, and poise. All Kitty ever wanted to be *was* Gloria because her face opened every door and warmed every heart, it brought the boys in slavering packs that she commanded with but one flick of her slender, graceful hand. It brought friends who wanted to be with her, to be part of her world, to bask in her glow that was golden. It was pure sunshine.

Kitty could remember on her fifteenth birthday, crying in her cake, hating the braces in her mouth (Gloria had naturally model-perfect white teeth) and the hair on her legs (Gloria never shaved her legs because hair didn't dare grow on those long golden limbs) and her face (no pouting lips or high cheekbones like Gloria) and her eyes (definitely not crystal blue like Gloria's) and just about everything.

"Come now," Mom had said. "Your sister's pretty, but so are you. Gloria has the kind of pretty that's going to get her in trouble, mark my words. But you got the kind the boys respect."

Kitty only wanted to be disrespected and have the wrong kind of pretty. Gloria went away to college and a pall fell over the house. Nothing Kitty did could warm up her parents the way Gloria did just by walking in the door. Whenever Gloria came home, they perked up and their blood started running again. Suffice to say, Kitty never formed a close bond with either her mother *or* her father. She cried only the acceptable amount when they passed within a week of one another via twin coronaries. As much as she seethed with envy over her older sister and boiled with jealousy, Gloria lit her up as much as anyone else. When Gloria came home, she did not ignore Kitty. She always made sure they had special time together. They watched movies, they shopped, they went to restaurants. Gloria always made sure Kitty felt special. Unlike everyone else, she never forgot about her and with that in mind, there was no way in hell that Kitty was going to forget about her now either.

But it wasn't going to be easy to succeed where the police had failed.

It was going to be dangerous whatever path she took. After what Ronny...or Piggy...had said to her in the dressing room, it seemed pretty obvious that they...or he...or *it*...knew who she was.

Back in Dayton, Kitty had accomplished everything she'd ever set out to do via sweat and hard work. Even as a little girl there was no quarter, no fear, no backing down from the most insurmountable odds. In a month, she was starting a new job in a new city far from the Midwest and before she opened a new chapter in her life, she planned on closing an old one. She deserved that and certainly Gloria's memory demanded it.

So here was another challenge. One with rules right out of the Twilight Zone.

But Kitty decided she would not back down.

Not yet.

8

The Bamboo Lounge.

Ten minutes to midnight.

"Now I ain't saying you're stupid, Ronny," Piggy said to the audience. "But when they emptied the gene pool, you were what was caught in the drain."

The drunks out there in that smoky, boozy haze were loving it. Laughing and slapping the tables. And the more they laughed, the faster the liquor flowed and the management liked that just fine.

"Night after night, Piggy, I sit up here and you insult me. Where will it ever end, I wonder?" Ronny said, shaking his head sadly. "You know, if I had a real job, I wouldn't need you."

Piggy laughed. "Sure, and if your dick worked, your wife wouldn't need me either."

The place broke up and Piggy grinned under the spotlight, feeding on it, packing away all the energy like a bear swallowing raw meat and storing it as fat. Ronny could feel him thrumming on his knee, sucking it up like a sponge, growing stronger, more daring...and he did not like it.

"What's with all these jokes about my wife, Piggy?"

The dummy kept grinning, wood that was aware. Wood filled with potential. "I'm just saying you gotta pay more attention to her, Ronny, that's all. Christ, she told me the other night she feels like Santa Claus."

"Santa Claus?"

"Sure, she only comes once a year."

"Now, Piggy…"

"I'm just kidding you, Ronny," Piggy said. "Your wife comes all year long. It's her way. Only the Big Bad Wolf has swallowed more pork than that lady. Hell, more men have been lost in her bush than in the Upper Amazon."

More laughter. Some drunken blonde in the front row, breasts spilling from her blouse, was clapping her hands and giggling in a high, piercing tone that cut through the guffaws like a straight razor. Piggy noticed her as did Ronny.

"Hey, honey, you like that?" Piggy said. "I mean, don't get me wrong here about Ronny…he's a good guy. But his wife has needs and all. She told me Ronny's pecker is so small, she has to blow pepper at it."

The woman giggled. "Pepper? Why pepper?" she called out.

Piggy said, "Well, she has to get the little bastard to sneeze just to find it."

The blonde could barely contain herself and some parts of her anatomy. In fact, she was too drunk to even bother.

"Sure, his wife tells me she feels neglected," Piggy said. "The only way she can get his dick hard is by sticking it in the freezer."

Applause now. A few whistles. It was hard to say whether Ronny was enjoying any of it or whether it was even part of the act or just random ad-libbing by Piggy…or Ronny.

"Tell me, sweetheart," Piggy said. "Are you a real blonde?"

Ronny sighed. "That's enough, Piggy. A gentleman doesn't ask such a thing of a lady."

Piggy held his hands up. "Listen, she's got blonde hair and I'm just wondering if the carpet matches the drapes."

"What's your name, honey?"

The blonde giggled and jiggled. "Mona," she said.

Piggy slapped a hand to the side of his head and everyone roared with laughter. "*Mona? Mona?* I tell you, folks, sometimes this shit writes itself. Mona, eh? I like that. Mona likes de bona. Giver her de bona and she starts to moana. Honey, in the land of gee-gee, you're strictly a blue light special."

Giggling still, the blonde said, "A blue light special? What does that mean?"

"It means your panties are always half-off."

A waitress went by with a tray of drinks and Piggy latched onto her. Gestured at her with his hand, whispered something to Ronny.

"Leave her alone," Ronny told his dummy.

"I was just wondering if you like 'em with big asses like that, Ronny. Hell, a girl like that? You put a corn cob in your back pocket and she'll follow you forever."

The waitress, a heavy girl, was smiling, but obviously not amused.

Piggy chortled. "Hey, I'm just kidding you, baby doll. Don't let me interrupt your work...go make that money, honey. You hear that, boys?" Piggy said to a group of salesman well into their cups. "Hear what she said? Five dolla, make you holla."

The drunks were loving it, even if the waitress wasn't. But she was new and she didn't know the ropes yet. The others knew you didn't go anywhere near the stage when Piggy and Ronny were doing their thing.

Piggy turned back to the blonde. "Honey," he said, "if you're in the mood for a good piece of wood, you let me know."

"Really, Piggy," Ronny said.

Piggy chuckled his dry laugh. "Hey, Ronny, I was thinking. Remember when you were a kid and they sold those snack cakes with the characters? Twinkie the Kid, Captain Cupcake, and Fruit Pie the Magician?"

"Sure. I recall."

"Well, they sound like a trio of pedophiles to me. Captain Cupcake liked the kids to lick his icing and Twinkie was always shoving his sponge cake in their mouths so they could taste his creamy filling. I bet when old Fruit Pie the Magician hung around grade schools, fruit pies weren't the only thing he made disappear."

"That's enough," Ronny said.

"Ah, you're still mad because I was ribbing you about your wife." Piggy put his hand next to his mouth like he wanted to tell the audience a secret. "Is it my fault his wife spreads faster than a brushfire? We're talking the champion sword-swallower of Cook County here, people."

"Why don't you quit picking on people," Ronny told him.

"Okay, okay." Piggy tapped a hand to the side of his head. "Hey, Ronny, you hear that Donald Trump was a test tube baby?"

"No, I didn't know that."

"It's true. Even then he wasn't worth a fuck."

This was the part of the show where Piggy started launching his one liners and the drunks absolutely loved it. Sometimes Ronny and Piggy would do three or four encores.

"Hey, Ronny, what do you call two lesbians in a closet?"

"I don't know. What do you call two lesbians in a closet?"

"A liquor cabinet," Piggy said. "You hear about the two lesbians that built a house?"

"No, what happened?"

"Well, it's pretty nice place…no studs, all tongue and groove."

It went on rapid-fire like that for maybe ten or fifteen minutes, but slowly but surely the laughs were milked from the crowd and Ronny was beginning to look uncomfortable. Piggy was getting that shine in his eyes, looking like Howdy Doody from hell.

"I think we're falling flatter than your wife's chest here, Ronny," Piggy said in that squeaking voice. "Maybe what these people want is real entertainment...should I give 'em something they'll never forget?"

Ronny licked his lips, swallowed. "No, ha, ha, don't do that."

The dummy seemed to be grinning. "Got a story for you, folks. Listen closely: Mama, Mama, Mama McBane, she had two children who caused her great pain. She was only happy after they were slain. She had another son who was completely insane. The doctors all agreed there was something wrong with his brain. He began to crack under the enormous strain. So, what could he do, old Ronny McBane? He delved in the darkness with knowledge arcane. What he did was wholly profane. He snatched two bodies from where they had lain. And now his life is one ugly stain. Isn't it shocking about Mama McBane?"

"That's enough!" Ronny cried out.

"Aw, come on, let's heat this joint up."

"Please, Piggy."

"You don't think they'd like me doing that?" There was an intensity to the dummy now, an edge there that was somehow sadistic, twisted, and not very funny. "Maybe they want me to pull a rabbit out of a hat? I can't do that, but I can pull something out of thin air that'll turn their hair white..."

"Okay, Piggy, stop that," Ronny said. "It's not very funny..."

"Oh, you're wrong, this is going to be a real hot one..."

Piggy was laughing and laughing with a shrill, scratching sound like fingernails on blackboards and it was loud, resounding, echoing, that malefic gleam in his eye.

The atmosphere of the Bamboo Lounge went from being drunk and care-free to somehow savage and deadly. Nobody was laughing, nobody was doing much of anything but squirming in their seats.

And about that time, somebody in the audience started screaming.

9

Danny Paul Regis looked like the sort of guy who broke legs for a living. He was big and meaty with a head like a cinder block, pumped with bad attitude and experience honed during twenty-odd years of swimming in the gutters and cesspools of the city. But as he liked to say, he knew dirt. He knew where to find it and what it smelled like, what it felt like when you got it all over your hands. There wasn't a rug made that he couldn't shake it out of.

And in his given profession as a private investigator, these attributes came in pretty damn handy. You wanted the job done? You wanted a guy who knew every nook and cranny of the dirty underbelly of the city? Then you wanted Danny Paul Regis.

So, when, after four days on the McBane investigation, Regis called Kitty Seevers to his office for a little chit-chat, she knew he had something.

"I'll tell you right off, Miss Seevers, that this whole McBane thing stinks bad," he said, pouring her a cup of coffee. "I've seen my share of bad in this business and what you put me onto here, it's *bad*. Oh, yes."

Maybe he expected Kitty to be shocked, but she wasn't. The deeper she dug on Ronny McBane the blacker and more rank the soil became. "Really?" she said.

"Oh yes, this one is really something. But don't take that the wrong way," Regis said, smiling now. "You chase enough adulterous housewives around, something like this really gets your gears turning. And that's no shit. I love getting my teeth into a freakshow like this."

For a lack of anything better to say, she said, "Well, I hope it didn't disturb you or anything."

Regis thought that was funny. "Disturb me? Ha, you can't disturb a guy like me, Miss Seevers. I've had my nose in human trash for too goddamn long. Now and then you can surprise me and sometimes you can piss me off and make me wish to God certain people weren't born, but you can't disturb me." He dismissed that with a wave of his hand. "What I found out was weird, but unfortunately, as yet, it's not bringing us any closer to your sister."

Kitty felt her heart drop. "No?"

He shook his head. "This is just preliminary stuff. Getting a feel for Ronny McBane you might call it."

Kitty said, "What did you find out?"

"Well first off, let's start with what happened over at the Bamboo Lounge a few nights ago. I'm sure you heard about that little tanglefuck…hell, the papers and TV ain't talking about much else in this city."

Kitty knew about it, all right.

And it was just another little gem for her collection: there had been a fire at the Bamboo Lounge. And, as it so happened, the fire started during the Ronny M. and Piggy show. Of course, the media wasn't seeing the implications of that. Most of the patrons escaped with minor injuries, but twenty of them were roasted to smoking husks. The media, true to form, were following the usual tract—overcrowding in the club, poor wiring, numerous safety violations. Ho-hum.

Kitty, however, had a few ideas of her own, and they were the sort of things she was afraid to admit even to herself. It was a coincidence, the reasoning mind would say, that Ronny and the dummy happened to be on stage. But some coincidences grew less coincidental the closer you looked at them.

She told Regis what she knew and he laughed. "Now are you ready for what really happened?"

Kitty swallowed. "I don't know...am I?"

Regis looked her straight in the eye. "You familiar with the theory of spontaneous combustion?" He saw that she was. "I was in on one of these investigations years back and that one was strange, but this is a little stranger. See, in a good many spontaneous combustion cases, the body will burn itself to cinders, yet sometimes the bed it lays on or the chair it sits on will remain un-singed. Go figure."

"Are you saying these people just burst into flame?"

"No, I'm not saying that at all," Regis explained. "It's the investigating cops that are saying it. Those twenty stiffs went up and didn't even melt the vinyl cushions on their seats. A few witnesses said they saw it...just those random twenty people all of a sudden billowing with smoke. By the time they realized what was happening, they were engulfed in flames."

Kitty nodded. "I see." Oh, this was getting better all the time. "Tell me, did anyone...any of those witnesses...happen to mention what Ronny and the dummy were doing as this happened?"

"As a matter of fact, that *was* mentioned."

"And?"

Regis shrugged. "Damnedest thing, really. These people are going up in flames, left and right...and Ronny's dummy is cackling like a madman. Ronny finally dragged the both of them off stage. Does any of that mean anything to you?"

But Kitty shook her head. "I guess not."

"Some people might call that kind of thing witchcraft," Regis said and said no more on the subject. "Crazy shit, all right." He opened a folder and sorted through some papers in there. "Well, to the case in question now. What I learned is a composite of public record and inside information, mostly gleaned from cops that were involved in the tawdry history of the McBanes. Now, for starters...did you know that the mother—Dorian McBane—was killed? And I'm not just talking killed here as in getting run down by a bus, I'm talking *killed*."

Kitty told him she knew about that. "A wild dog or something."

"Yeah. That's what the coroner put down in his report. But that was old Biggs, he'd write anything down to save his ass some paperwork. Anyway, yes, that was the official version, like it or not. But I talked to one of the investigating detectives and, well, Mama McBane, she was chewed-up pretty bad. But if it was a dog, well then it was one smart pooch because it locked-up on its way out."

Kitty ignored the implications of that. "And she died from these bites?"

He shrugged. "More or less. Couple the bites with trauma, shock, blood loss...yeah, they did her in, all right. That was about ten years ago. Just a few years after Ronny McBane got himself into the ventriloquism racket." Regis sat down, drumming his big fingers on the desktop. "The family had a history of trouble long before the mother's death. Apparently, when Ronny was five or six years old, the father committed suicide. Ronny found him swinging in the basement. After that, it seems that Dorian—Mama McBane—kind of lost touch. Became a hardcore Bible-thumper. I talked to one of her old neighbors, a woman listed on the police report as being the first person on the scene after Ronny found his old man. She told me some pretty wild stories. Lot of it was what you'd expect, you know, Dorian turning into a right pain in the ass knocking on doors and handing out leaflets. The usual. But some of the rest of it? Christ on the cross, you gotta hear this."

Kitty figured she'd have to, too…not that she really wanted to.

"Get this," Regis said, enjoying the dirt of other people's lives maybe a bit too much. "Dorian told this neighbor lady that the father—his name was Robert—was some kind of witch or warlock, whichever, that he descended from what she called 'witch-folk' back in the old country…Scotland, I'm guessing. But this neighbor lady said that was crazy, because Robert McBane was a pretty good guy. Maybe his ancestors were a little loopy, but he was okay. She never saw him stirring any cauldrons or flying on any brooms. He was a good neighbor and a good father to the kids. He came from money, but he was no good with it himself. One failed business venture after another. The neighbor lady figured this is why he hanged himself. She also added that if there was a witch in the McBane family, it was the mother…Dorian was pretty screwy long before the old man's suicide. And if his failed business dealings weren't enough incentive, the shrew he was married to completed the picture.

"Of course, that wasn't Dorian's version of events. She said the old man was born 'of tainted blood' and Jesus had compelled him to take his own life. That was what she told the neighbor lady a few months after he was gone. Regardless, there were certain facts in the neighborhood that everyone knew. And one of them was that Dorian McBane was a mean, spiteful old bitch. Everyone felt sorry for the kids without the old man around. It was common knowledge that Dorian did not like children and that she took the belt to her own any chance she got. And after the old man made for the pearly gates? Well, Dorian not only found religion, but she began abusing those kids. There's some pretty wild tales there, too, bits about her locking them up in the attic, not letting them go outside, burning them...you know the bit. It never changes with these animals."

No, Kitty supposed it never did.

She sat there, thinking it over. She'd gotten real good at swallowing madness in raw chunks, letting it bubble away in her stomach while her brain tried to digest it without throwing it back up. It left a vile taste in her mouth, but thus far she'd been keeping it all down. Thus far.

"What happened to the children?" she asked.

"A series of coincidental mishaps that don't sound real coincidental when you put them in the same basket." Regis sorted through notes on his desk. "Okay. Ronny had a sister named Molly. A little sprite of two when she died. Suffocated in her little bed...or was strangled. Things get a little murky there. The coroner put it down as suffocation...but the cops I talked to, well, they said the kid's window was wide open and they had suspicions that somebody had reached in and throttled her."

Kitty tried to swallow, but couldn't. Jesus, what kind of monster had Dorian McBane been? "What about the other child?"

Regis nodded. "He was six. Just turned six as a matter of fact. Dorian, the neighbor lady told me, was real hard on this one because she said he had the devil in him. A real terror. The neighbor lady confessed that he was just all boy, but Dorian had told her that she feared he was contaminated by the McBane ancestry. So, about a year after Robert McBane hangs himself, the little girl suffocates and about a year after that, the boy is found in his bed with a light cord wrapped around his throat. The cops figured it could have been accidental...kids do crazy shit."

Kitty sat there, thinking, feeling it coming over her because she was seeing things now, feeling dark truths invade her and seeing connections where there could not or should not have been any. In a weak, airless voice, she said: "What was the boy's name?"

"The boy?" Regis smiled the cold, dead grin of a beached fish. "The boy's name was Freddy, but everyone called him 'Piggy'."

10

Kitty swallowed two Valiums just before eleven that night and washed them down with two double vodkas. Her head wasn't right and she wondered if it ever would be again. She had come to Chicago to fill a hole in her life, to possibly get some closure on Gloria if that was even possible, but now that hole was bigger than ever before, so big she was afraid that she would fall into it and never get out. *Ronny M. and Piggy. Ronny M. and Piggy.* The words kept running through her mind until she thought she would scream. *You honestly don't believe for a moment that Ronny's dummy is his dead brother, now do you? All that witchcraft business is insane and you know it.* No, she didn't really believe any of that, but what she did believe in was Ronny's madness which was so complete he might decide to name his dummy after his dead brother and commit crimes in its name.

But what about what Bascomb said?

Could some evil intelligence make a vent dummy that was kept in a coffin filled with black, wormy grave earth sit up and smile, start talking to you in the tormented voices of your mother and father—

No, no, no. That was Bascomb supposedly quoting Eddie Bose who wasn't in his right mind anyway. She'd already more or less dismissed Bascomb as a nutjob. None of those things he said could be true. The dummy killing Bose, then killing his dog, then murdering his wife. Fantasy. It was only when Kitty linked it with what Regis had been hinting at and the possible spontaneous combustion at the Bamboo Lounge that she began to get the cold sweats.

You said there was a common thread to all this. You said it right from the first. Are you prepared to follow that thread even if it means looking at something that might tear your mind out like moist roots from soil? Are you willing to do that and accept the fact that even if you walk away from all this you can never be the same person again? Bascomb told you to walk away. Maybe it's time to do that.

But no.

That would mean walking away from Gloria and her love for her sister could not allow that. If there was a thread, she would follow it. And when she reached the end she would snip it.

Once again, as the alcohol and Valium began to make her limbs slow and her mind slower, she laid all the evidence out and tried to make sense of it. This is what she came up with: Bascomb was crazy, Danny Paul Regis was spouting hearsay and local gossip, and Ronny McBane was very possibly a dangerous lunatic that had killed Gloria.

Kitty thought these things, arranging them carefully, sorting them out in her mind, smoothing out rough edges. And it was as she did so that a fear of her own began to creep in that she was utterly wrong. That she was over-rationalizing things and that, in this case, could prove to be very dangerous.

All her life she had not shrunk from anything.

She faced all problems and challenges head on. Even though she knew that this was the point in a horror movie where you hoped the heroine would have sense enough to leave well enough alone, she wasn't about to do that. She didn't believe in witchcraft or ghosts, but there was definitely a common thread here as she had thought all along. Rational thinking aside, when you laid it all out end to end starting with what happened in Ronny McBane's childhood and the unnatural dummy with the most disturbing of names and ending with the fire at the Bamboo Lounge, then the evidence was more than a little damning. Possibly circumstantial, but it was there. And the only way to prove or disprove it was to follow the thread to its source.

This is what Kitty thought as she drifted off on that night of revelations.

11

She came awake just after three with a sense of invasion. Her eyes blinked and then blinked again and she had the most unnerving sensation that they had been open for some time, perhaps peering around the room and watching the play of shadows along the walls as her mind continued to drift along in dream. Her lips felt dry. She licked them with a tongue that felt thick and ungainly. She could see the digital clock. The numbers flickered from 3:02 to 3:03.

She felt paralyzed.

It was the vodka and the Valiums. They always said not to mix them and she rarely did except on those nights when her mind would not shut down and her body remained tense from the day.

The sense of invasion did not lessen, it deepened.

There was a foul odor in the room that she associated with dankness, with subterranean crypts, with corpse-orchids rotting in mortuaries. It was a high, sweet smell and it did not belong there in the dead of night.

She tried to move, to reach over to the lamp and turn the light on, but her arms were leaden. Just the effort of lifting even one of them two or three inches left her feeling exhausted.

Listen.

Terror began to expand in her throat and she could not swallow it back down. It filled her chest with icy needles, traced its way down her spine like cold fingertips. The shadows seemed to shift and rustle about her. She heard them make slithering sounds. Something was in the room with her and she could hear it breathing with a low, rasping sound. It knew she was aware of its presence. She was certain of it. It was there, hiding in the darkness like some malignant little goblin waiting to jump out at her and press its mold-smelling mouth to her lips. It was there and it wanted her to find it.

And then she did.

With a tremor of fear that seemed to drain the blood from her vitals, she saw it. It was not in the room at all. It was outside the window. The curtains were parted and she could see Piggy floating out there like a wraith, staring in at her with a malevolent and hungry gaze. His dummy legs and dummy arms were spread out like a high diver dropping from the sky, like some engorged human fly buzzing at the window pane. He moved up and down as he floated as if he was hooked to wires being gently manipulated by a puppeteer.

The window began to slide open.

Oh no, oh no, you're dreaming. You're just dreaming.

He came drifting through the window, light as a column of gas, and she heard the subtle *click, clack* as his little shiny black shoes touched the floor and bore his weight. He stood at the end of the bed, his puppet face pale as funeral lilies, his hinged jaw opening and closing. His eyes were huge, bloated white like boiled eggs. And his voice, when it came was scratching and dry: "*I've come as I said I'd come, Kitty. I've come to show you tricks. I've come to perform for you. I've come to eat your pretty pussy.*"

Kitty thought she screamed.

Her mouth opened and a dark silence blew out of her but it only echoed in the depths of her skull. Piggy was rising up like a patch of mist. He was drifting above her, arms spread out. She could smell a vaporous stench of dank rot coming off him. It

55

was chill like the breath of a freezer. She could see his dummy hands, impossibly white, the nails blackened and splintered like they had been clawing at the lids of caskets. In her head, there was a thick liquid humming and she could hear his squeaking voice just beneath it telling her in grisly detail what he was going to do to her and what he had done to her sister.

She tried to scream again but all that came out was that same airless sibilance blowing past her lips.

Her limbs would not move.

Her body was heavy, rubbery, immobile.

He came down upon her and she could feel the grave-cold of his hollow weight. Her nightgown was stripped away from her bare thighs but not by anything as crude as searching fingers but by something like a hot wind. There was nothing beneath the nightgown. She had slept naked like that since a teenager, enjoying the freedom from confining underthings.

Piggy buried his face between her thighs and his wooden mouth was like thawing meat, his teeth needlelike as they were dragged over her vulva like the claws of a cat. He began to suck and chew on her, piercing into her soft tissues and laying her open. His tongue was a sliver of ice as it penetrated her, lapping and licking deep inside her as the mouth sucked and slurped, filling itself with her blood that steamed in his glacial aura. The agony was unbelievable, exploding in her head in white bolts but still she could not move and she knew it was more than Valiums and vodka by that point.

She was pinned down and made weak by the force of Piggy's mind.

Lapping like a kitten with a bowl of milk, he rose up again and came down upon her, his puppet face smeared with her vaginal blood, his breath like exhumed coffins. He made obscene, almost animal-like grunting and groaning sounds as he entered her with a member that felt refrigerated, swollen and probing. It was long and burning cold like an icicle had been shoved up her.

"*You have such a sweet, sweet, pretty pussy,*" he whispered into her face with that vile, mossy breath as he came and then came again, filling her with a cold sap, what seemed gallons of it that overflowed her channel, flowing her over thighs and seeping into the mattress in a bubbling, snotty goo. "*Next time I'll show you another trick and I'll fill another hole…*"

Then he was gone.

The room was empty of all but the commingled stench of him and the webby gush of liquid he had inundated her privates with. She could feel it drying, thickening, becoming a cool-warm jelly that encased her, glued her legs together, and pasted her arms to her sides. She could barely breathe. It was like pine sap that held her, capturing her in amber like an insect. She felt herself sinking in it, drowning in sticky, phlegmy depths. It would cover her completely, gumming her eyes shut and filling her nostrils and flowing down her throat and filling her lungs, gallons upon gallons of slimy, ectoplasmic semen. Her mind raged, her mouth tried to scream, her body tried to thrash…but in the end, she was pulled down and down, buried alive in darkness.

It was later when her eyes opened.

She could hear a constant, racked sobbing and it took her a moment or two to realize that it was her own. She could still feel the dummy's ejaculation all over her, only now it had dried into a viscous, gelatinous emulsion that felt like cooling candle wax, rivers of animal tallow sealing her up and holding her forever in place. Her crotch burned, her thighs felt like they'd been scraped by forks. She could taste vomit in her mouth and bile in her throat, all the while smelling Piggy's discharge which stank of gangrenous drainage, untreated wounds and running pus.

You were raped, you were raped, you were fucking raped! Do you hear me? You were raped!

But no, no, no, she would not and could not accept that. Her head thrashed from side to side on her sodden pillow and this was the first time her body seemed capable of any voluntary motion. The tears ran and the whimpering sounds bubbled from her mouth.

Do you hear what you're saying, you silly bitch? Raped? Raped? RAPED? By a fucking dummy? A puppet? A ventriloquist's doll? Are you totally out of your pea-brained fucking mind?

And she was. Oh yes, most certainly. The desecration she had suffered had kicked her mind right out of her skull. Even now it was circling her brain like a dying planet, trying to find its way back in, trying to cement itself to her psyche and her id and bring the terra firma of reality with it.

Raped...raped.

She closed her eyes listening to her own sobbing.

When Kitty opened them again, the sunlight was coming in.

She leaped from bed, still feeling the cold violation of the dummy, smelling his charnel breath and feeling his icy member sliding into her. She stumbled into the bathroom. He had been chewing on her. The pain was a distant memory, but an insistent one. She examined herself carefully. There was no blood, no ache of rape, only that pervasive psychic defilement that she could not shake.

It was a dream. You dreamed it all.

But she could not convince herself of the same because she could still hear his voice and feel the violation. Piggy was a dummy. Dummies did not rape women (or men for that matter). She kept telling herself this as it slowly began to fade from her mind. She repeated it under her breath again and again and she would have really believed it if it hadn't been for the fact that the window was still open.

And she knew that she had closed it last night.

12

And it was that afternoon, after a long and surreal day in which she was haunted by what might and might not have happened the night before, that she received an envelope by special courier. It was from Charlie Bascomb. There were several sheets of paper in there. On one of them, Bascomb had scribbled: *I found this in Eddie Bose's room. It was in a drawer. I never showed it to the police. When you're done reading it, please burn it. C.B.*

That was all.

The rest were written in a rambling, spidery script that seemed to roam all over the page. And from the looks of them, they were the final thoughts of Eddie Bose, one-time ventriloquist and full-time lunatic.

Kitty began to read, feeling something tightening inside her from the very first line.

> *To whom it may concern,*
>
> *If you have this in your hand, then I'm pretty much toast and that's not very funny and it's not intended to be. I just want you to know some things that happened to me. Some things I can't bear to admit to another living soul, because if you didn't know this already, people think I'm*

nuts. Maybe they're right and maybe I have a good reason.

The subject of what I'm going to tell you about is the McBane family and before I start spreading the dirt on this old Scottish clan, let me just say that I brought most of this on myself. And if it wasn't for Ronny McBane, I wouldn't be even as alive as I am right now. Understand that. So, let me be brief here on account I don't think I have very much time. Ronny McBane is a ventriloquist as I was once. Ronny had a most unusual dummy, one that was like no other and so, true to form, I had to know about it. I had to know what made it different and why. And that was the stupidest thing I've ever done. Curiosity killed the cat? Sure, but this cat wasn't killed outright, but one day at a time. Makes no sense? Of course it doesn't. Just keep in mind most think I belong in a straightjacket. That might make this an easier read. Long story short, I was obsessed. I had to know how this dummy of Ronny McBane's could move by itself, could speak when he was nowhere near...and the expressions on its face, my God. Well, suffice to say that this dummy was the sort of unintentional bait no self-respecting vent artist could refuse.

And I took it, I sank my teeth into it. God help me, but I did.

Yes, the bait was offered and I bit. I never thought it would bite back.

Okay, board the crazy train with me because here we go. I was so obsessed that I broke into the McBane house. It was one of those tall, rambling old Victorian nightmares up in Edgewater. You lived here long enough, you've seen them, no doubt. Big, ass-ugly monstrosities, busy and confusing with towers and gingerbread and wrought-iron fences, all that crazy 19th century shit that makes you think the architects wandered out of a Lewis Carroll book. Popular on Halloween, but just goddamn odd the rest of the year. Anyway, you don't want to hear about that. Point is, I broke into the McBane house. I jimmied a window in the back and went in. I'm not going to tell you what I saw because I don't trust myself. I could not have seen what I thought I saw. All I know is that whatever I looked at, it burned my soul to cinders, filled my brain full of ashes that are still blowing around up there. I'm hoping this makes sense, because most days I have a pig of a time stringing together two or three coherent sentences. Well, like I said, I saw things there that turned my brain to jelly. Drove me right over the edge. Not only that, but gave me something of a stroke that paralyzed my left side to the point that I have no feeling there.

Onwards and upwards.

Ronny found me laying there in the upstairs hallway and he got me out of there. I was a wreck. I had pissed myself and my hair was streaked with white. I could not speak. I could barely think. But Ronny carried me out and got me into his old car, took me home. It was a pretty valiant, selfless act on his part, because that act of kindness must have cost him dearly. I'm sure he paid a terrible price for it.

From who? Well, I'm not ready to go there just yet.

The McBanes. Quite a bunch. Just as I researched Ronny and his dummy, I researched the McBane clan. Why? Because something told me his family history was pertinent. At least, I like to tell myself that. The truth is, people, yours truly is what is known as a compulsive-obsessive. I've always been that way. When I get into something, I just don't get my feet wet, I dive right in and touch bottom. And this time, well I touched bottom, all right.

Here goes. The McBanes. Well, you know how some people say a house has a history if there has been some dark events in its past? Well, the McBanes are a family with a history. You can trace them right back to Medieval Scotland where they were hell on wheels and, yes, I do mean that literally. The McBane's closet is full of skeletons and the problem is, unless you slam that door real quick, they keep rattling out. You see, the McBanes have a rich and colorful history replete with pirates and bootleggers, slavers and murderers, executed criminals and more than a

few 18ᵗʰ century graverobbers of the Burke and
Hare ilk. But, to balance things out, branches of
the McBanes have also produced clergymen,
politicians, and decorated soldiers. There was
even a 20ᵗʰ century McBane who became
something of a soda pop baron in the UK.

But we're not interest in those people.

We're interested here in the McBanes as
witches.

Yes, you heard me right: witches. As in black
cats and broomsticks. For some of the earliest
references to the clan involve accusations of
sorcery, necromancy, and the conjuring of
poltergeists. Most of it is pretty sketchy, but
during the infamous North Berwick witch trials
of 1590, the McBanes became very popular. The
entire clan was indicted by the state for a bevy of
unbelievable, awful crimes against "God and
man". Some of the charges are as follows: calling
plagues of rats into the city; causing fields to go
fallow; having commerce with demonic familiars;
calling up the spirits of the dead and putting
them to nefarious uses; the making of waxen
conjure dolls; the selling of "ungodly, profane"
charms and philters; the defiling of graves to
obtain bones and corpse flesh from which they
supposedly constructed awful little puppets or
dolls which they sold to locals for the uses of
revenge and murder. Well, you get the picture.
They were accused of calling up storms and

spreading disease and pestilence, all kinds of things. And not just the adults, either. For the McBane children were named as well.

Now, it is well-known historically that Scotland is second only in barbarity to Germany for the sadism of its witch trials. Most of this was accomplished under the auspices of the Presbyterian clergy and was considered savage even for that savage time. Well, back to the McBanes. The children were apparently shuttled off to monasteries and the like, but the adults were tortured viciously. The Spanish Boot and Witch's Bridle, Caspie claws and thumbscrews, the ordeal of the pins and pincers. The entire family was "put to the question" as they said back then. In the end, some eight members of the clan were burned alive, two others strangled and then burned, and a few more simply sent to prison.

What the hell does this have to with anything?

I'm getting there. Just understand that the McBanes have been mixed up in this business for centuries, whether real or imagined. A 17th century source claimed that the family was "cursed of God" and "contaminated by a degenerate heredity" and so forth. Earlier references mention that the McBane children, at birth, were of a "most loathsome appearance, displeasing to the eye". Was this some possible hint to their origins? This "look" was known as the "McBane taint". By their first birthday, the children had outgrown that unwholesome appearance...but it makes you wonder if there was some sort of unspeakable interbreeding in the family's past.

Now, let's jump to the present. Let's imagine this "foul seed" being carried from generation to generation. Now, that night Ronny brought me home, a drooling wreck, he told me many things and I think he told me them as a warning of what was to come. He told me that his father was not a necromancer like his father and his father's father. He had no interest in such arcane matters as harvesting the spirits of the dead, which had been a family tradition for too long to remember. When Ronny's grandfather died (Ronny surmised) his father burned all of his old books and diaries, to cleanse the family once and for all of that morbid stain.

But he didn't get everything.

Sometime later, he took his own life. And that, I think, was the catalyst for Ronny's domineering, demented mother to go on her rampage. You can check the criminal records on that. Suffice to say, the three McBane children, without their father's protection, were brutalized and abused by their mother. They were whipped, locked in closets for days on end, burned with crosses (this after their mother found Jesus), put on starvation rations, beaten, lashed...well, you *can full imagine the rest. And the point? Because, yes, in their mother's violent dementia there certainly was a point. And that was because the children were McBanes and carried what she called "the filthy, godless stigma" of their cursed blood within them. They were filled with devils and said devils had to be purged, forever and ever, Amen. The end result was that Ronny was the only survivor. His sister suffocated (supposedly) when she was two. His brother was strangled (accidentally) with a light cord.*

And this left only distraught, alienated, unbalanced Ronny who liked to talk to dolls, to create personalities for them. When he was a teenager, he discovered some family heirlooms up in the attic (as he was not allowed to leave the house) his father had not burned. One of them was a notebook kept by his grandfather. I will not say the rest of what he told me. Maybe I can't say it. Now, who wouldn't want their dead loved ones returned to them? What kid of Ronny's age and mental aberration wouldn't consider following extreme paths when a notebook showed him the way? Dear Christ, who wouldn't have done what he did? Torn up by grief, alone and frightened and out of his mind? Who wouldn't have? And especially a disturbed boy like Ronny.

When Ronny carried me up to my apartment that night, he said something to me. He told me there were blasphemies in that notebook, horrible, diabolical methods for doing things unthinkable to a sane mind. That to practice necromancy was to rip asunder a barrier that was not meant to be crossed. For your loved ones (their souls) were unreachable, but that there were other things out there, hideous things, malign and decayed intelligences waiting to be born, to be called down from the black spaces beyond. And these things...they were hollow and wicked, unborn and evil...yes, things, shades, shadows that were never meant by the Creator to inhabit flesh and blood, things that were never meant to be born.

Crazy? Yes, you think it, too, and I don't blame you. Then again, I don't care and why should I? You haven't seen what I've seen and you haven't felt what I've felt. Your mind, your soul has not been defiled by these malignant intellects. My number is almost up and I welcome death, it's better than what I live with day in and day out, this madness. You are not haunted by a dummy possessed of infinite diabolic darkness. You do not wake to find that it has chewed the flesh from your numb leg. You do not feel it biting you in the dead of night. You do not see that grotesque, macabre corpse-puppet drifting outside your fourth story window, tapping at the glass, scratching it with those bony fingers. You don't have to hear it creeping beneath your bed or calling your name from the closet. And you don't know what it's like when it comes, not alone, but with another...a cackling, squeaking pestilent thing with sharp teeth and a lurid baby-doll face.

I hope you never have to find out.

But if you do, if you are named as I have been named by that horrible dummy, then do what I should have done right from the first: burn the McBanes out. Burn that house and let the fire destroy everything inside. It will be a cleansing and a welcome relief for Ronny McBane who has suffered for his sins again and again. A purging. But whatever you do, stay out of the attic. Don't go up there like I did. Don't make that fatal mistake.

The letter ended there.

It was enough. What more did Kitty really need now for her charter membership in the Lunatics of the Month Club? It was all there. A perfect and oddly seamless madness like a glittering garment tossed aside, just waiting to be picked up and worn.

The temptation to feel it against her skin, leeching her mind of life and light, was almost too much. And still, that slightly mangled and mutilated voice called reason was calling out to her from some dung heap at the bottom of her psyche and it was telling her to go slow, for other than a few very impressive parlor tricks with a ventriloquist dummy, she had utterly no evidence to go on here. Nothing but hearsay, wild tales, unconfirmed facts gathered by a somewhat shady private detective, and a letter from a madman.

And was that enough?

I have one more thing, she thought in her desperation. *I have a dream I had last night that I feel was not a dream at all but something else. Maybe not an actual physical rape, but definitely a psychic and spiritual rape. I have that. And I can't dismiss it or get past it.*

Still, she wasn't 100% convinced, but she was so close to that yawning ebon gulf of overwhelming, irresistible superstitious acceptance that a good breeze could have knocked her ass over the brink.

I think, she thought then, *I think that, yes, I believe. It's crazy, but I really do.*

And maybe it wasn't the evidence she had, but something indefinable. Some esoteric, mystical sense of acceptance. Some race memory perhaps that recognized the signs, the smells, the sights, and recalled them, told her in no uncertain terms that, yes, this is real, and you'd better watch your step, girl, for here be dragons. Here be things you cannot fathom nor hold in the palm of your hand, but things that can hold *you*, crush you, kill you quicker than a knife across the jugular. For there was certainly an undercurrent here and whatever it was, it had already made up her mind for her.

Ronny McBane was not just a ventriloquist.

And Piggy? He was a dummy like an Egyptian mummy is a hand-puppet.

So, with all that in mind, there really was no way to avoid what came next.

13

She had barely finished reading the letter and absorbing all it had to say when her cell rang. She answered it hesitantly, grateful to be able to talk with another sane, reasonable person, but terrified that she might hear the sound of teeth chattering when she answered it.

But it was Danny Paul Regis. "Charlie Bascomb's dead," he said.

Kitty sat there on the edge of the bed, staring numbly at a print on the wall of some peasant boy balancing a bowl of fruit atop his head. She felt panic seize her, squeezing her throat to a pinhole, her heart galloping in her chest like it was trying to burst free and run. Her hand shook so violently she could barely hang onto the phone.

"Kitty?" Regis said. "Kitty? Are you all right?"

She breathed in and out, forcing herself to mellow incrementally. If she got this wigged out over some bad news, how the hell did she think she'd be able to handle the McBane clan when the time came for—

"Kitty?"

"I'm okay," she said. "A bit of a shock, that's all. What happened?"

"Suicide."

She almost started laughing. She did not think suicide was in the least bit amusing, but *suicide?* Really? *Really?* Is that what the police had come up with? Well, of course they did. They knew nothing of the McBanes and the foul seed of evil they carried within them. They knew nothing of what Ronny had done out of desperation and madness. They didn't know what he had called back from beyond the pale of the grave.

"He jumped out of his apartment window, apparently. Eight stories. Not much left when he hit, if you know what I mean."

"He jumped, eh?"

"Yes."

"I guess the question is," she said, "did he really jump or was he thrown out the window or compelled to take a swan dive?"

"Kitty...what the hell are you talking about? You're not making sense."

"Oh, I think for the first time in these many weeks I'm finally making perfect sense."

Regis was no fool. There was no need to spell things out for him. He understood what she was thinking because he had thought many of the same things himself and he knew exactly what sort of dark paths it would lead you down. "You think Ronny did it. Or, better, you think Piggy did."

"Don't you?"

"That's not rational."

She chuckled. "I have a feeling there are things in this world that are not strictly rational by our definition, Mr. Regis. I think they're rare, but they do exist. And now and again some very unlucky idiot like yours truly gets a glimpse of them." She paused a second, trying to catch her breath which was coming a little fast, she realized, making her sound just a bit less than rational. "And you know what happens to these idiots? They either become agoraphobic nutbags that are so terrified of the world that they're afraid to leave their houses or they end up in intensive therapy *or* in padded rooms where they're fed a steady diet of lithium and thorazine for the rest of their tortured, pathetic lives. Then there's the other variety. The types that are not about to bow under. Their own fear and anxiety pisses them off to the extent that they fight, they track their fear to its source and destroy it before it destroys them."

Regis sighed. "And I guess you're in the latter category?"

"Yes. And that's why I'm going to the McBane house."

"Kitty, listen to me. That's dangerous as hell. If even half of this shit is true then you're walking into a snake pit. Even if this witchcraft shit is total B.S., Ronny McBane might be psychotic."

"And I'm going to find out."

"Let me go with you."

"No. You've done enough. Now it's up to me. I'm the one who's been wronged and that means I'm the one who has to put things to right."

14

Bathed in the glow of the full moon above, Kitty stood on the sagging, expansive porch of the McBane house and knocked and knocked. The place was pretty much as she envisioned: very old and decrepit, shingles blown loose and siding flapping, windows boarded-up and doorways warped.

She stood looking up at the ramshackle monstrosity, feeling the poison bleeding from the foundation. This was not a house, this was a casket, something yanked from moldering gums like a rotten tooth. It was too tall and too narrow, a leaning oblong rectangle cut from night. There were windows up there, shadow-riven cavities that refused moonlight and starlight and anything bright or revealing. A house of mystery and dank secret and no light dared reveal its dark glory.

In one pocket of her leather jacket was a flashlight, in the other her little .32 automatic. She knew how to use it. She'd been through a defensive firearms course and she had complete conviction that she would not hesitate pulling the trigger if it came down to it.

The door finally opened a crack...and just when Kitty was thinking—gratefully—that maybe nobody was home. The door opened an inch, two, no more than that and she saw a sliver of Ronny McBane's face, one wide, unblinking eye.

"*You*," he said, as if she were some ancestor that had wandered from its crypt to stand threadbare at the threshold.

"What do you want here…you can't be here. Just go away…you don't belong here."

And she knew that, but she said, "We need to talk, Mr. McBane. It won't take long."

He looked behind him. "Just go away…please just go away."

"I'm not going anywhere," she said, her steadfast resolve still holding even though her guts were beginning to feel warm and soft.

"Go away!" he snarled in a whisper. "Just go away from here!"

And then there was another voice in there, something splintered and creaking and eldritch: Piggy. "Let the lady in, Ronny. She's come for something, can't you see that? Don't be disrespectful now. Do you hear me, Ronny? Be a good boy."

"No, please…"

"Let her in, Ronny. She's come for something and we must see that she gets it."

And for one unstrung moment, Kitty thought that the voice had something of a feminine caliber to it. The way a mother might speak to her son.

The door opened and she walked in, right past Ronny who glared at her with unmasked hatred. But did he hate her or did he just hate the indomitable will of modern women in general? Because sometimes, such qualities could be an attribute, but other times the keys to doors best left bolted.

That's not hate, Kitty thought then. *Can't you see it around his eyes? In the pale line of his mouth? That's fear. Ronny is terrified. And not for himself, but for you.*

Inside, it was chill and damp as she imagined such houses must be. For regardless of the romanticism of such places, the real truth was that they were drafty and dank. Kitty could almost smell time here, the slow parade of decades the old house had seen. She could smell, too, the wormy woodwork and mildewed wainscoting, the dirty carpets and yellowed wallpaper. But there was something else…a brooding, pervasive sense of contamination, of spiritual rottenness. There was no getting around it and no denying it. What this house was and what it contained made her flesh creep.

But forward-thinking and liberated as she was, Kitty kept moving through the foyer and into a high-windowed sitting room.

Piggy was in there.

His trunk was leaning up against the wall, lid open, like a mummy sarcophagus. He was sitting on the end of a flowery, dirty green sofa that might have been a fashion statement in its day, but was now just an eyesore. He was dressed in the same velvet cranberry suit coat as the last time she'd seen him, spidery hands curled in his lap like the claws of a raptor.

Kitty looked from him to the night pressing up against the windows. "Hello, Piggy," she said, trying to sound amused.

He said nothing, playing the perfect inanimate little dummy.

She smiled thinly. "I said, hello, Piggy."

She had only seen him beneath the stage lights and the dim dressing room bulbs, never in full electric light before. His face was painted very white, like that of a circus clown. The eyes were huge and abnormally round, shining like newly-minted nickels. Kitty could see where his jaw was hinged, how the paint was flaking to gray at his throat.

Then the jaw dropped open with the sound of dry lips parting, the eyes blinked and blinked again. "Pretty, pretty Kitty, come to pay us a call. Did you bring your pretty pussy with you?"

Kitty tensed. She felt her hand grip the .32 in the pocket of her leather jacket. It was no dream last night…at least, no dream in the ordinary sense. She calmed herself. First, she would find out about Gloria, then she'd destroy that grinning imp, she'd chop it into pieces and shove it in the fireplace, watch it burn.

"I'm glad you've come here," Piggy said. "I knew you would sooner or later. Your curiosity would get the best of you and lead you shivering and helpless into my lair."

"I'm hardly helpless."

The dummy cackled. "Innocent as a babe, as a squealing piglet put to the knife. That's what I like about you."

Kitty did her best to remain unfazed even though being in close physical proximity with this little horror was making the flesh at her belly crawl in waves. "I'm waiting for a dirty joke, Piggy. Have you run out of them?"

"I'm contemplating the dirtiest joke of all, pretty pussy, with you as the punchline."

"I can't wait to see it. Does it have anything to do with men jumping out of windows?" Kitty said, feeling the anger rising in her.

"Oh, we're beyond all that, Ronny and I," Piggy said, his eyes impossibly black and wet like drowning pools. There was something behind those eyes or, and maybe better, a *lack* of something. "We're contemplating new heights since our performance a few days ago…aren't we, old chum?"

Ronny looked confused, then nodded, then laughed. If it was meant to be a reassuring laugh, it missed the mark completely. The sound that came out was forced and shrill like somebody on the verge of a nervous breakdown.

He passed by Piggy and sat in a recliner. "What do you want here, Miss Seevers?"

Kitty looked at him, showing no fear. "I think you probably know. I think you probably know why I came around the first time, too."

"No," Ronny said. "You're mistaken, so why don't you —"

Piggy started cackling. "C'mon, Ronny. She wants to know about her sister...she wants to know about Gloria. You remember Gloria, don't you? Pretty Gloria? You better confess, tell Kitty all about her...don't you think? After all, Pretty Kitty has a gun in her pocket."

"That'll do, Piggy," Ronny said, still thinking, even after all that had happened, that he could make this all sound like part of the act. "Yes, I remember Gloria. She worked with us...but just for a short time. We couldn't pay her what she wanted, so she left."

Piggy started cackling again and it was hard to imagine a more unpleasant sound. It was high and fragmented, that laugh, echoing and perverse. The laughter of a child molester. And he did not laugh as men laughed. His hinged jaws snapped open and shut in rapid succession, the laughter billowing up darkly from somewhere deep inside of him. If Kitty had ever suspected that Ronny was actually throwing his voice, she knew better now.

"Shut up!" Ronny shouted at him and meant it.

And the dummy did. Its head was thrown back, its jaws hanging open, eyes staring at the ceiling. One moment it was filled with something dire and malevolent, and the next it was simply a wooden dummy, vapid and vacuous.

"I just want to know about my sister," Kitty maintained, trying to tell herself she was not frightened, not held together inside with spit and frayed wire. That the invasive madness of this place was not possessing her. "That's all I really want, the rest of it I don't care about."

"I already told you what I knew," Ronny said, an edge to his voice now, his breath coming hard.

"Hee, hee. I told you that lock of hair would bring the pretty pussy running into our arms," Piggy said. "And was I not right?

Did I not prophesy it as I now prophesy the unpleasant end of pretty, pretty pussy?"

"Stop it!" Ronny cried. He turned to Kitty. "I don't know anything about your sister! I don't! I don't!"

Kitty felt cold from the balls of her feet to the top of her head. It was all planned, all arranged. She had been manipulated from the first. The bait was thrown out and she had taken it and now she was firmly hooked. Piggy had foreseen it all. Now he would count on her fear, on mental degeneration settling in. But this, she decided, is where his plans would go to hell.

Piggy's head swiveled in their direction, mouth still gaping. "I think it's too late for that, Ronny. Our dear, pretty Kitty has been talking to people, hearing the things they had to say and believing them…careful now, Ronny, no sudden moves…she has her hand on the gun."

And it was true. Her hands were in the pockets of her leather car coat and the right one was gripping the little .32 automatic tightly now. Piggy seemed to know it.

"If she wants to kill me," Ronny said, completely indifferent, "then let her kill me."

"Oh!" Piggy laughed. "You silly, silly boy! You'll ruin all the fun!"

But Ronny wasn't having fun. "Go ahead. Shoot me."

"Well, you heard the boy, Kitty, better just do it…then we can be alone. And you do want to be alone with me…don't you?"

"Stop it," Ronny said.

"Tsk, tsk, old boy," Piggy said in a patronizing tone. "You see, Kitty. He doesn't want to talk about girls. Boys and girls and the things they like to do in the sweet, heady darkness. Hee, hee, hee. Girls make him uneasy. They make him so uneasy that sometimes he—"

"Shut up, shut up, shut up!" Ronny cried, on his feet now, hands balled at his sides, then up against the sides of his head, pressing and pressing. "I don't want to hear it! I don't want to hear any of it! So just shut up!"

"Shut up? Sure, kid, I'll shut up. I'm good at shutting up. I've been shut up in a lot of bad places. Kind of like I was shut up in the family vault until you—"

"Stop it!" Ronny shouted at him, his eyes welling with tears now. "*Just stop it! I want it all to stop!*"

"Oh, but I won't stop it. Remember how it was? Did they tell you how it was, Kitty? Ronny can...he was there. Why don't you tell the girl, Ronny, tell her all about it. How you used to come and see your brother in the vault, talking to him and missing him...and wasn't it all so sad? Boo-hoo, said the Jew."

"Stop...it..."

The cackling again, eerie and discordant. "No, no, no, Ronny, I won't. I won't stop any more than mother would stop when she suffocated little Holly with the pillow or when she wound that light cord around my chubby little neck. I'll never forget that...*and neither will you...*"

Kitty was losing her mind now; it was just too much. She brought out the gun and leveled it at Ronny, said in a trembling voice: "Where is my sister? Where is my goddamn sister?"

Ronny turned on her, hair hanging in his face, lips pulled in a snarl. He was mad, completely unhinged. "Get the fuck out of my house!"

Kitty brought the gun up. "I'll use it," she said.

"She will, Ronny," Piggy said. "What are bad girls made of? Ha, ha, sugar and spice and plenty of lice! You'd better take her to her sister..."

But Ronny put his hands to his head, sobbing and whimpering...and then he froze, stood up straight, began walking in a tight circle like a toy soldier, finally dancing in a sprawling, loose-limbed shuffle like a marionette controlled by strings from above.

"He'll take you now," Piggy said. "And when you get back, then we'll discuss your future, pretty pussy. Or the lack of the same."

15

Silently, Ronny turned away and Kitty followed at a discreet distance, the gun still up and ready. He led her to the stairs and moved up them mechanically, each foot placed carefully before the next came down. He waited for her up there, his back to her. Not threatening, not anything really. Just lifeless and dull, an automaton being worked by the unseen hands of Piggy.

She came up behind him slowly, feeling the maleficent blood of the house seeping into her now like plague, feeding into bone and marrow, nerve ending and muscle fiber...infesting her with its toxins which were positively black and rancid. She could almost feel her soul putrefying.

Upstairs, it was even worse.

It was a puppet graveyard. There were fine threads like cobweb plaiting the walls. It drooped from the ceiling in filaments and fibers and loose nets. There were things tangled in them, objects that she first thought were the mummified remains of children but they were dolls...no, not just dolls but puppets and vent dummies, some whole and others represented only by stray limbs and dangling baby doll heads, cleaved torsos. They were everywhere in the corridor. It was a jungle of cocooned doll parts. Gray, flaking faces webbed by spiders. Chubby hands speckled with mold. Legs furry with accumulated dust. Heads fixed to the walls in blind, eyeless rows, torsos hanging in clusters. And all of it woven and threaded together like beads sharing a common string by that network of gossamer material, shrouded in fine plaits of the stuff like the bodies of insects in a spider's lair.

"What? What is all this?" Kitty said, her entire body trembling now.

There had been a barely-suppressed terror right from the first, of course. Just coming to the house was frightening enough...but the longer she had been in there and the deeper she penetrated its nameless mysteries, the more the house gripped her and held her, getting its hands around her throat and its fingers along her spine. And when she saw all those puppet and doll parts hanging in that web—if web it was—the terror no longer circled her heart like hungry wolves in the darkness, it leaped on her. It rode her and embraced her and flooded her with fright. She could feel it making her belly weak and her limbs numb, the fine hairs at the back of her neck rising like hot wires.

"I said," she breathed, "*what is this?*"

But Ronny did not answer and it was as if he were incapable of the same. He just stood there like some blind, mindless mannequin as Kitty made little shrieking sounds as she ducked under the reaching marionette hands and bumped into a clown puppet whose face had been gouged with a knife. Turning, she stumbled into a collection of doll heads and let out her first real scream. Some lacked eyes, others were cracked open, still others were near-melted, their flesh bubbly as if they had been in a fire. The heads swung back and forth around her like Japanese lanterns in a wind. A huge white moth abandoned a doll's empty eye socket and six or seven leggy black beetles dropped from the straw-dry locks of another into her hair.

She stumbled into Ronny who was no more alive than the things hanging around her, tearing the beetles from her hair and stumbling into the wall, her fingers brushing the numerous slack-jawed puppet heads and she screamed again. For their faces did not feel like thermoformed plastic or carved wood but like warm, living flesh.

Gathering herself, trying to tell herself that she was not lost in the expressionistic tangles of a fever dream, she said, "Show me. Goddammit, show me."

Ronny paused before a door and backed slowly away into the shadows of the hallway. Strands of web broke against his face, drooping figures and doll anatomy swaying around him. He found a corner and faced into it like a child waiting for a dunce cap.

The door.

It was warped in its frame, the knob dirty and tarnished. Kitty did not know exactly what was behind it, yet she seemed to know very well. There was a hot panic in her belly slowly chewing up her insides, eating her from the inside out and she had all she could do not to scream.

The door opened.

There were no electric lights on in the room, only a candle flickering at a bedside table, throwing greasy shadows along the walls. Kitty looked back to Ronny. He had not moved. He didn't seem capable of movement. She went into the room and saw that there was a shape on the bed, a shape beneath a graying linen sheet. She watched it, tense inside, her heart hammering painfully.

She stepped over there, taking her time.

Her movement in the room made the candle sputter, its flame leaping and shrinking. The shadows were coiling around her like worms. For not the first time, she sensed what might have been very subtle movement under the sheet…practically nonexistent. Maybe a drawn breath…an arched finger.

Kitty reached out, grasped the edge of the sheet, felt something electrical feeding up through her fingertips and gathering in her guts in a buzzing knot. Sucking in a sharp breath, she yanked the sheet free.

And something screamed.

Something jumped.

Something writhed and shuddered and hissed.

Kitty fell back, fear punching into her, but did not go down. Her eyes were showing her things and her lips were mouthing, *no, no, no,* and her mind seemed to close like a hothouse flower. Because what she saw…it was far worse than anything she could have imagined.

There was not a body under the sheet, there were only *parts* of a body.

A left leg, a right arm, a head. Placed in sequence as if they were awaiting to be sewn to the torso whenever it arrived. The limbs were corpse-limbs, not doll or dummy parts. They were covered in a seamed gray flesh that had torn open in spots, revealing bones and metal armatures. The elbow was fitted with a plastic swivel, as was the knee.

And they should have been dead, but like the head, they were alive.

The leg was jumping and kicking, the arm thrashing and the hand slapping the filthy mattress beneath. The head was whipping from side to side on the pillow. It was Gloria's head…or had been. Her wheat-colored locks were splayed over the sheets, her jaw hinged, her left eye missing and her right fitted with a glass ball onto which a tiny pinprick pupil had been painted. Part dummy and part corpse and all lunacy.

Kitty felt a scream empty itself from her mouth, but it was not a scream, not really. More of a wracked, broken sobbing that rattled up the chimney of her throat, taking everything with it but the instinct to survive.

The head rolled and fixed her with that one lurid ping pong ball eye. The waxen, lumpy face grinned at her. *"Look upon me, sister,*" the voice said, not a voice really but an airless whistling noise, wind blown through a pipe. "*Look upon me, look upon me, look upon me…*"

And then those hinged jaws fell wide open and a piercing shriek came out that scraped up Kitty's spine like a knife blade.

She turned and the door slammed shut.

The .32 was in her hand. She jerked the trigger, bullets punching straight through the cheap-paneled door and Ronny cried out. She thought she heard him fall out there. The door was not locked and she went right through it, tripping over his collapsed form and scrambling free.

All of the doll and puppet parts and bodies were in motion on their strings, swinging and shuddering. The jaws of puppet and vent dolls were opening and closing, glass eyes rolling in sockets.

Kitty heard a sliding, dragging sound.

Something was coming down the hallway: *slap, drag, slap, drag.*

She tensed, her hand shaking as it gripped the .32. The inside of her mouth felt like it had been oiled with cooking spray and maybe that was the taste and texture of overwhelming horror.

Something came out of the darkness and it looked like swollen gray sack inching its way toward her. But it was no sack. It was Gloria's torso. Its remaining hand would slap the floor, pulling it forward and then repeating the process, the right leg dragging behind it like a vestigial limb.

Piggy was sitting in the hallway, cross-legged. He was grinning as he always grinned, shadows coveting that abominable doll's face, his eyes bright and yellow and glittering like moonlight on wet pavement.

"You have to understand things, Kitty, because you do want that…don't you?"

And then he was telling her things, as she wildly debated whether to shoot the dummy or its master or the dragging carcass. He was telling her about graves and tombs, about little boys rotting away in satiny caskets. About their brothers stealing their corpses, taking them into high, secret rooms and using techniques cribbed from moldering notebooks. Fitting little boy corpses with special puppet mechanisms, swivels and pivots and hinges. Stripping away dead flesh and replacing it with wax and plastic artifices. Saying words over those dead little puppet boys and hoping, hoping the words would bring their brothers back to them...and how they did. How they brought something back, but how it was not the soul of a dead little boy, but something else entirely. Something that had been scratching at ethereal barriers for eons, something with hunger, something looking for a home and a body to steal...

But Kitty would not listen.

She put three more bullets into Ronny and he stopped moving. She put one through Piggy's chest, but it caused him no inconvenience.

"You don't really think you're getting out of here alive, now do you?"

And Kitty ran down the hallway away from him, into another room. Because in a room there would be a window you could jump out of. But in that room, the window was boarded and the door slammed shut behind her. There were candles glowing in there, too. And what they revealed was a tiny casket, the sort you might fit a doll into.

And Kitty wasn't really surprised by that point when the lid swung open and a little girl dummy sat up in there like a Jack-in-the-Box. The little girl was Ronny's two-year old sister and her face was smooth as porcelain, flaking away to bone in spots and dotted with black mold. It had no eyes. The hinged jaws snapped open and closed, a demented, reedy little girl voice said: *"Baby doll, baby doll, baby doll, baby doll, baby doll..."*

It kept repeating this, fleshless arms held out, blackened fingers splayed. It wanted to be scooped up and held.

Kitty supposed she might have screamed.

The candles went out and she emptied her .32 into the darkness, at those places in the room where she could hear something small and rat-like scurrying, crawling, sliding along like a slug. And then teeth bit into her ankle. She cried out and took hold of that hideous little corpse-doll, feeling the flesh coming off in her fingers like sloughed snakeskin. But she held on, yanking its body away and hearing a rending, wet snap, realizing that the head was still biting her. Still hanging on with those little needling milk-teeth and that she had cast the body against the wall, where it had shattered...but refused to die. Screaming then, Kitty pounded that little head with her fists until it began to come apart, until only the jaws held. Then they fell away, clattering like wind-up chattery teeth in the darkness.

Above, in what must have been the attic, there was a rumbling noise. The ceiling shook, dislodging a rain of plaster and dust. Something was up there and it was angry.

Kitty found the door, the little corpse-doll's remains still clawing away in there, looking for something to hold and lead to those teeth.

Kitty found the knob and fell out into the dimly-lit corridor.

16

The sane thing to do would have been to escape, if escape was even possible by that point.

But Kitty was not leaving.

Despite all the other horrors she had drunk deep of this night, she could only see Gloria. What was left of her. What they had done to her. She would never know the torment Gloria had endured in her final hours and she did not want to know, but she was going to put things right.

Somehow, she had to.

She remembered what Eddie Bose had written:

...burn the McBanes out. Burn that house and let the fire destroy everything inside. It will be a cleansing and a welcome relief for Ronny McBane who has suffered for his sins again and again. A purging. But whatever you do, stay out of the attic. Don't go up there like I did. Don't make that fatal mistake.

The attic.

That was the key. That was the beating black heart of this nightmare and this is where she was going to go because this is where the puppeteer was that Bose had mentioned. That was where he must have gone that night that Ronny found him and brought him home. What was up there was the very thing he dared not speak of.

But Kitty had no weapons.

The .32 was empty.

She was going to go up there anyway.

Whatever the attic held, whatever noxious and cancerous spirit brooded in darkness up there like a fatal egg coming to term, she was going to it now. She would face it and she would not fear it. Ronny McBane and Piggy and, yes, even the horrid little Baby Doll were connected to the thing that waited above. Like mittens connected to sleeves by strings, like hands fused to wrists by bones, like souls knitted to flesh by ethereal filaments, they were but appendages of a greater, more colossal and unspeakable horror.

Find it. Run it to ground.

All she had for weapons was her anger, her rage…and her bare hands.

Kitty held her hands out before her, fingers splayed like the tines of divining rods, feeling for those threads and finding them. The puppeteer was near. Hiding and skulking, she could feel him or her or *it*. Sense their unease. Their fear.

Those drifting strands of webs were everywhere in the moonlight seeping in from high windows. Kitty reached out, knotting them in her fists like reigns and leads, pulling herself along. Following those strands and cords to where they might take her. They were guide-ropes in her hands, skeins of worn yarn leading back to a nightmare quilt that had been knitted so long ago. The quilt that was a puppeteer, a witch and a soul-eater, the sort of thing that suffocated children, a plague-blanket, a winding sheet forever adrift in search of bones and meat and biology.

Where? *Where?*

Kitty kept going, her eyes lit like green gemstones, a burning core of energy blazing in her belly. She felt the threads, traced them with her fingertips. They jumped and arced like sensitive nerve ganglia as she neared the brain itself. The threads were growing thick as tree roots in her hands now.

They felt moist and fleshy and vital. And Kitty followed them, her own moon-struck shadow like a stalking cat moving along the facade of dirty brick and lathing showing through the rotted wallpaper of the McBane house.

The corridor angled to the right and the webs grew thicker here. Just ahead, a door opened momentarily and she saw something distorted, something patchwork, something hideous like a face woven from damp wicker staring out at her.

Then it disappeared and the door slammed shut.

I've got you now. You can't hide.

The door itself was hanging by one hinge and she pushed it aside, tearing through webs strung tighter than cotton candy, clawing through the spun insulation of dead spiders and into the narrow stairwell itself.

She had not dropped the threads.

She still clutched them tightly and now they were agitated, leaping in her fingers like live high-tension wires, snapping and jumping, slithering like the tentacles of something that ate ships in misty, lost seas. Now she dug out her flashlight and exposed the inner viscera of the stairwell. But it was no stairwell as such with dusty joists and warped water-stained ceilings…it was a casket. The walls were made of quilted satin that was badly discolored and bleached, grayed and mildewed. Ropes and nets of spiderwebs dangled overhead, great winding plaits of them set with the mummified bodies of puppets and deadwood vent dolls. The stairs were covered in what seemed millions if not billions of dried insect carapaces heaped like barnacles on a ghost ship.

Kitty's mouth was dry, her heart was pounding. She started up the steps, dead insects crunching beneath her boots like October leaves. The flashlight shook in her fist.

Keep going, you have to keep going.

She breathed in revulsion and exhaled resilience. Her heart was strong and her soul was rigid. But she was scared. The fear was thick and white knotted in her belly, spreading out and coiling around her chest in thick bands. She could scarcely draw a breath. But this was to be expected, she knew, for fear and dread and irrational terror was the language of this house and the thing that brooded in the attic. She couldn't give in to it. Those myriad shrunken, embalmed figures dangling in the webs…their sightless eyes watched her like the eyes in antique paintings in old farmhouses. Their driftwood and winter-dead limbs brushed against the top of her head. Their agonized mouths seemed to scream her name.

Overhead, dangling and swaying from the roof of the stairwell, there were limbs now. Not doll limbs, but dozens and dozens of blue and black corpse limbs…arms and legs, sometimes just hands and feet…all hanging from the webwork above like sausages in a butcher's window. They were putrescent and bloated, shuddering with the action of pupa and larva within and speckled with millions of buzzing meatflies.

More games. Just games. Hallucinations. Images projected into your mind. Ignore them.

Kitty went up through them, all that cold, crawling beef brushing her face and head, cold fingers trailing across the nape of her neck. They were a forest and as she pushed through their marble masses, they began to swing and slap into each other, casting creeping and morbid shadows all around her. Feet that walked into space and great hands that clutched.

Then she was beyond them and into the attic above which was spun and wreathed and roped together by cobwebs. It was the lair of a funnel web spider decorated with more puppet parts and doll heads which whispered to her. Like the ones downstairs, these were living disembodied things with wiggling fingers and mouths that made mewling, wet sounds.

Right away, the temperature dropped.

Kitty saw her breath and felt ice on her face. The threads in her hand were greasy and coiling, set with pink-mouthed suckers that tickled her palms. Yes, she had arrived. A numbness spread from her fingertips to her elbows and then subsided, leaving a maddening tingling just beneath her skin.

The webs moved around her, brushing her face and slithering over her back and climbing her legs. By y the time she realized what was happening, they owned her. A webby mesh covered her and she clawed it free just in time to see the haunter of the attic in all its multiform madness.

She screamed. Screamed like she had never screamed before, or, maybe had never *allowed* herself to. It came up from her guts and echoed out of her anguished soul with volume.

An abomination came down the network from its high roost.

It came to embrace her.

It was a carcass riven with worms, then a thousand spiders mating and then something like a man vomiting a green-flecked infant from his mouth that sprouted a dozen bulb-headed, malformed fetuses.

Kitty saw what looked like an immense, bloated fetal spider propelling itself towards her on a dozen wooden puppet legs, its underbelly hung with milk-swollen pink teats. It was hairless and cream-white, bulbous and distorted, great holes eaten through it in which vermiform parasites squirmed and coiled. Rising from what might have been deemed the forward thorax was the upper body of a woman whose head was hung with draping cobweb locks, the face beneath set with bulging eyes of black glass and a suckering oval mouth. It was not one thing, but many things—animal flesh married to doll parts and human anatomy—stitched up into a common whole and the intricate suturing was like lacework spread out in loops and whorls.

Beyond screaming by that point, Kitty had dropped to her knees with absolutely no memory of doing so. Her heart was pounding so hard that it was like a drum beating at her temples. The level of blood in her body seemed to fall into her feet and everything above that point went weak and tottering in the presence of the thing that was poised to press its blubbery white lips to her throat and suck away her life.

Oh God, oh dear God, not like this, I don't want to die like this.

But she was going to die and she knew it. She was going to die shrieking away her mind as Gloria had and she was powerless now to stop it. This horror would pull her apart and hang her cooling remains in its web...if it didn't decide to add them to its own heaving mass, that was. And the only possible compensation for any of it was that she *knew*, she knew what this thing was or, and better, *who it was.*

Dorian McBane.

This was the deranged apex witch that had started the entire ball rolling by abusing her children in the first place which led to the murder of Freddy and Molly which led to Ronny's dementia and paranoia which led him to finding that awful notebook which led to the resurrection, more or less, of his brother and sister as corpse-puppets possessed of malignant minds from beyond time and space which led to them reanimating their wicked mother as this chimeric, grotesque monstrosity...which, essentially, was her true self externalized.

As that wailing, enraged face came to kiss her life away, Kitty saw that it body was shivering, rolling like jelly, dozens of blisters bulging from the flesh and popping to reveal baby doll faces which were grim caricatures of the children she had murdered. Pale, agonized faces, embryonic yet identifiable. The heads lashed from side to side, mouths opening with a strident mewling like the hungry cries of newborn rats.

With each generated head, the Dorian thing itself squealed with pain.

Up close, Kitty could see that while its face was bone-white and fleshy, it seemed to be composed of bloody filaments of tissue in constant flux, oozing and puffing out, deflating and reconfiguring itself in some vain attempt to be anything but what it was.

I'm sorry, Gloria. I fucked up. I tried, but I fucked up—

That's when the cannon boomed.

The sound of it in the vault-like attic was so deafening that Kitty cried out and covered her ears.

Dorian's face imploded like a can crushed in a fist, from jawline to forehead just a wriggling mass of bloody strings sinking into a craterous ruin. Wailing louder than ever, she scurried back up the web.

Kitty saw Danny Paul Regis standing there.

His tough demeanor was shaken, his face strained and his eyes delirious with fear. But he did hesitate. He carried a twelve-gauge pump loaded with flechette rounds that were essentially razored bits of steel that pulverized their target on contact. He fired four rounds into Dorian and she literally exploded in a wailing mass of tissue and bone, trembling armature, hinges and swivels that filled the web and continued to move and shake.

He dragged Kitty down the stairs and into the corridor and that's when Piggy attacked.

17

He hit Regis with incredible force, the shotgun flying from his hands and tumbling down the stairs. Piggy's jaws clamped around his ankle and bit down with a moist snapping of bone.

Kitty saw it happen.

She fell, panting and staring and oddly numb. She did not think anything or feel anything. All that was gone. Fear was a memory and now she was insane, too, so the playing field was leveled. Snakes do not fear other snakes.

Piggy.

Fucking Piggy.

No more pretense of a dummy, he came walking down the hallway toward her. And what a walk: stiff-legged, shaking, clownish. Kitty lay there, hearing the dummy coming, *click-clack, click-clack*. He brought a black stink of rifled coffins and open graves, a miasmic stench of buried things roiling with worms. When he was close, very close, so close she could see that the face was not painted on, but maybe rubber or leathery flesh or both, Piggy smiled, lips pulling away from yellowed teeth. Biting teeth.

"*Kitty, Kitty, Kitty*," he called out in a dust-dry, cracking voice. "*You made my plans go all shitty. So now I'm going to rape you just a little bitty. I'm going to bite your titties and then I'll chew on your slitty. That's what I'm going to do to my pretty little Kitty.*"

The dummy reached down for her with those skeletonized fingers, the eyes blazing with a cold intelligence that was bitter and noxious. *"You killed little Baby Doll. You killed little Baby Doll and she'd waited so long, long, long to be born…just as we all waited so long…"*

And then Kitty came up with a scream, flattening the dummy, feeling it under her, writhing and flopping, clawing and snapping its jaws. But she was too smart for it, far too smart and that evil voice did everything it could to terrify her. It became the voice of her dead mother and then Gloria, then a sniffling baby and a slithering thing and a cackling witch and a slobbering rabid dog. Its face became the faces of corpses, of child-eating things and breathing things from closets, it took on a goatish visage and then it was just Piggy. Piggy, eyes yellow and baleful, fighting and screeching and trying to bite her, but she was too strong.

Taking the dummy by the ankles, Kitty swung it into the wall.

And then again and again and again.

Most of its face was shattered by then, its hinged lower jaw hanging by a thread of wire. Kitty dragged it down the steps and into the sitting room. And this is when the thing that occupied the corpse-dummy began to roar and thrash. And that's how Kitty knew it was afraid.

Really afraid.

Because there was one thing it feared more than anything else and that was being expelled back into the formless, drifting blackness it had come from. That's why she dumped it in the trunk and snapped the lid shut, set the locks.

It was trapped and it knew it.

Kitty dragged the trunk out the door, thinking of the darkest, deepest, coldest place she could deposit it. She helped

Regis out to his car and put the dummy's trunk in the back. Before she left, she made sure the house was burning bright.

In the backseat, the dummy shrieked and clawed inside the trunk.

"What're you going to do with it?" Regis asked, pulling off a cigarette, each bump the car went over making him grimace.

"I want to put it somewhere very dark where that thing can be alone with itself for an eternity," Kitty said.

Regis smiled. "I know of a flooded quarry out in the middle of nowhere. About two-hundred feet deep if it's an inch."

"Your leg?"

"Can wait. First things first."

Kitty drove out of the city. She did not think she would smile again for some time to come, but inside, where it mattered, she was grinning with immense satisfaction. Gloria was at peace now.

About the Author

Tim Curran is the author of the novels *Skin Medicine, Hive, Dead Sea, Resurrection, Hag Night, Skull Moon, The Devil Next Door, Doll Face, Afterburn, House of Skin*, and *Biohazard*. His short stories have been collected in *Bone Marrow Stew* and *Zombie Pulp*. His novellas include *The Underdwelling, The Corpse King, Puppet Graveyard, Worm*, and *Blackout*. His short stories have appeared in such magazines as *City Slab, Flesh&Blood, Book of Dark Wisdom*, and *Inhuman*, as well as anthologies such as *Shadows Over Main Street, Eulogies III*, and *October Dreams II*. His fiction has been translated into German, Japanese, Spanish, and Italian.

Find him on Facebook at:
https://www.facebook.com/tim.curran.77

Bibliography

Novels
Afterburn
Bad Girl in the Box
Biohazard
Blooding Night
Cannibal Corpse, m/c
Clownflesh
Dead Sea
Doll Face
Graveworm
Grim Riders
Grimweave
Hag Night
Hive
Hive 2: The Spawning

House of Skin
Long Black Coffin
Monstrosity
Nightcrawlers
Resurrection
Skin Medicine
Skull Moon
Terror Cell
The Devil Next Door

Novellas
Blackout
Corpse Rider
Deadlock
Fear Me
Headhunter
Leviathan
Puppet Graveyard
Sow
Tenebris
The Corpse King
The Underdwelling
Toxic Shadows
Worm

Collections
Alien Horrors
Bone Marrow Stew
The Brain Leeches and Other Eldritch Phenomena
Dead Sea Chronicles
Here There Be Monsters
Horrors of War
Zombie Pulp

Curious about other Crossroad Press books? Stop by our
website: http://crossroadpress.com
We offer quality writing
in digital, audio, and print formats.

Subscribe to our newsletter on the website homepage and
receive a free eBook.

www.ingramcontent.com/pod-product-compliance
Lightning Source LLC
Chambersburg PA
CBHW022041170626
46808CB00003B/1315